Praying Drunk

PRAYING DRUNK

stories,
questions

KYLE MINOR

Sarabande  Books

LOUISVILLE, KENTUCKY

No part of this book may be reproduced without written permission of the publisher. Please direct inquiries to:

Managing Editor
Sarabande Books, Inc.
2234 Dundee Road, Suite 200
Louisville, KY 40205

Library of Congress Cataloging-in-Publication Data

Minor, Kyle.
[Short stories. Selections]
Praying drunk : a collection of stories and questions / Kyle Minor. — First Edition.
    pages cm
"These stories are meant to be read in order"--T.p. verso.
Includes bibliographical references and index.
ISBN 978-1-936747-63-4 (paperback : acid-free paper)
I. Title.
PS3613.I657A6 2014
813'.6—dc23

2013040118

Cover design by Kristen Radtke.

Interior layout by Kirkby Gann Tittle.

Manufactured in Canada.

This book is printed on acid-free paper.

Sarabande Books is a nonprofit literary organization.

This project is supported in part by an award from the National Endowment for the Arts.

The Kentucky Arts Council, the state arts agency, supports Sarabande Books with state tax dollars and federal funding from the National Endowment for the Arts.

for

Don Pollock, Kirby Gann,

Matt Bell, Neil Smith,

Jen Percy, Tom Quach,

and

Okla Elliott.

If I lose my demons, I will lose my angels as well.

—Rainer Maria Rilke

Note to the reader:

These stories are meant to be read in order.

This is a book, not just a collection.

DON'T SKIP AROUND.

CONTENTS

I.

"I Wish My Soul
Were Larger Than It Is"

THE QUESTION OF
WHERE WE BEGIN

WE BEGIN WITH THE TROUBLE, but where does the trouble begin?
My uncle takes a pistol and blows his brains out.

Now we may proceed to the aftermath. The removal of the body
from his bedroom. The cleanup. The reading of the will. The funeral
in West Palm Beach, Florida. The woman he wanted to marry, taking the ring he gave her and putting it on her finger after the death.

But this beginning is not satisfactory. The mourners are now
parsing their theories of why. Did you know that he was brain-
damaged when that city dump truck hit him twenty years ago? Look
at his children grieving in the front pew of the funeral room. Why
wouldn't they visit him except when they wanted his settlement
money? Had his settlement money run out? And where is his
ex-wife? Why couldn't she love him enough to stay with him (for
better or for worse, right?)? Do you think it's true he was physically
violent with her like she told the judge?

Now we're thinking the trouble doesn't begin with the
big event. It's the grievance that led to the big event. Perhaps he
wouldn't have killed himself if his children had more demonstra-
bly loved him. Perhaps he wouldn't have killed himself if his wife
hadn't left him.

Perhaps his wife wouldn't have left him if he had never been physically violent with her.

Perhaps he would never have been physically violent with her if his brain chemistry had not been altered by the city dump truck that hit him twenty years earlier. So perhaps we begin at his old house, in the morning, him buttoning his workshirt, smoothing the patch that bears his name on the pocket of his workshirt. Perhaps our story is about the workings of chance. What if he had stopped or not stopped this particular morning to get coffee? What if he had ordered two hash browns in the McDonald's drive-thru instead of one hash brown, but had to wait a little longer for his order, since only one hash brown was ready, and the second hash brown was still in the fryer?

But this, chance, isn't story. Chance doesn't satisfy the itch story scratches, or not chance entirely. Story demands agency. But whose? My uncle was no dummy. Why was he a common laborer? Why didn't he go to college?

Now we're parsing family-of-origin stuff. His mother and father. My grandmother and grandfather. She was a lazyish homebody who wore a muumuu in her trailer every day of her life I knew her unless it was beauty shop day. He was a wellpoint foreman who spent his child-raising years as a raging alcoholic who yanked the curtains off the walls. She didn't finish the eighth grade. He only finished the sixth. Maybe if she had thought school was important, my uncle might have gone to college, got a white-collar job, missed the dump truck. Maybe if he hadn't made my uncle sleep in the bathtub almost every night, my uncle might have slept better, been more alert in school, been encouraged by some teacher to go to college, got a white collar job, missed the dump truck, married a different woman, had different children, earned until he was eighty.

What if his mother and father had never met and married at all? What if sperm and egg had never met? Or what if sex was not, as my grandmother once asserted, a nasty thing forced upon her in the night, but rather a thing of love and passion? Or what if something had been different in Owensboro, Kentucky, where they met in a roadhouse? What if the idea of love somehow transformed my grandfather into a man who could declare that for his seventeen-year-old bride and their children-to-be, he would never touch the bottle again? If we change a variable here and there, my uncle doesn't lock the doors, lie down on his bed, stick the pistol in his mouth, and blow his brains out.

And if we can lay some causal blame upon my grandparents, what about their parents? Who was this Kentucky coal miner Billy Ray Charlton who kept making babies with women and then making babies with their sisters? What did it mean for my grandmother, the little girl she was, to sleep in winter on the floor of a drafty shack in the mountains near a clear-cut someplace? Who were the men her stepmother aunt brought home at night after her mother died?

Again we enter into the questions of chance and existence. What if a mine collapsed upon Billy Ray Charlton before he could make his way from the bed of one sister to the bed of another? What if he mistimed a subterranean dynamite fuse and blew himself to death? What if there was a weakness in the rope that was used to lower his cage from the surface of the mountain to the mine shaft below? What if the rope snapped, and he was crushed among the others in the bent metal, or run through by some sharp stalagmite? No Billy Ray Charlton, no Edna Jo Mason. No Edna Jo Mason, no uncle. No uncle, no suicide.

Thinking this way, we're soon thrown upon the exigencies of history. What if that proto-Charlton had not got on the boat from England and sailed somewhere toward the southern colonies? What if somebody a generation or two later had not heeded the call west, not settled in some Appalachian hollow and made somebody who would make somebody who would make Billy Ray Charlton, who would settle even farther west, in Owensboro?

What if the winds had not cooperated in 1588, and the English had not won the Battle of the Spanish Armada? Would anyone in North America be speaking anything but Spanish at all? Would anyone in England?

And what if the Taino Indians had known enough to find a way to kill and silence the genocidal murderer Christopher Columbus in the year 1492? Would the continent have been overrun by Europeans?

And what if the Angles, Saxons, and Jutes had not imposed their barbaric Germanic languages upon the Celtic Britons at the point of a sword? And what if the Roman Empire had not grown fat and lazy and become overrun by Vandals? And what if, on some prehistoric plain somewhere, the people *Homo sapiens sapiens* had not triumphed over their Neanderthal neighbors?

And now our trouble—the inciting incident of the story of my uncle's suicide—has moved past the historical and into the cosmological. It could be, as the ancient Finns say, that the world was formed from an egg that was broken. Or it could be, as goes the diver myth of the Iroquois, the earth was covered with muddy water at the beginning of time. When a Sky Woman fell from above, she was caught by water animals who made a home for her by diving into the seas to bring up mud, which they spread onto the back of Big Turtle, and this mud grew into the great landmass. For all I know, maybe the Incas were right when they spoke of an earth covered with darkness until the god Con Tiqui Viracocha emerged from the present-day Lake Titicaca to create the sun, the moon, and the stars, and to fashion human beings from rocks he flung toward every corner of the world, and he kept two of them, a man and a woman, by his side in the place they call the navel of the world.

But this of course is the story of my uncle, and if on his terms—a man who came of age in Florida in the 1960s—we're talking origins, we're talking either the Big Bang Theory, in which the universe began from some ultra-dense and ultra-hot state over thirteen billion years ago, which predated the fabric of space and time and has continued to expand outward ever since, or, more likely, we're talking the literal rendering of the Book of Genesis he would have heard as a child in the Southern Baptist church: In the beginning God created the heaven and the earth. And the earth was without form, and void; and darkness was upon the face of the deep. And the Spirit of God moved upon the face of the waters. And God said, Let there be light: and there was light. And God saw the light, that it was good: and God divided the light from the darkness. And God called the light Day, and the darkness he called Night. And the evening and the morning were the first day.

By one way of thinking, we've entered into a cold intellectual exercise of technical cause-and-effect, which couldn't be any more distant from the story of a flesh and blood man who wore a mustache his entire adult life, who never felt comfortable in a suit, whose smile was crooked after the accident, whose voice was believed by his nephews to be unsettling and weird. We're laying blame and skipping all the important stuff, like how it seemed the last time we saw him that he was finally turning it around, that this woman he was with was a good thing. She was a jeweler. He had bought a house. Together they were buying a commercial building. You could see a future where she joined him on the cross-country road rallies he occasionally raced. In time you could see him becoming a man who didn't complain about losing the love of his ex-wife and his children every two or three hours. You could foresee a big-screen television in the living room, a big black leather sofa, satellite channels, the premium package with the college football games from the western states and Formula One auto racing from Europe and Brazil. You could see that the ring he had bought her would soon enough be on her finger where he wanted it instead of in her purse where she could think about it. You could see her negotiating with herself over time, talking herself into marrying him. That was why they were so often coming to visit my parents' house in the months before he died, no doubt about it. She was willing him a close-knit family so she could join it.

At the funeral, somebody said what always gets said, which is all things work together for good to them that love God, to them that are called according to His righteousness. And I wondered, if the story started there—because that's the classic *In the beginning* scenario—what did that say about a God with agency sufficient to create everything and set it into motion, and apathy enough to let it proceed as an atrocity parade?

Or what does it say about me, the god of this telling, that I have to take it to these dark places? Because it is within my power to do what I now want to do, which is to start the story with the more pleasing trouble Henry James prescribed—the trouble of he and she, and how they met, and how he toured her jewelry shop, and how she showed him how to shape a ring, set a precious stone, finish a setting, display the thing under glass, move a delicate hand in the direction of the display case, match a ring to a finger, watch a man and woman walk away wearing the symbols of their love. And couldn't I end it somewhere in the world of promise, he and she beside a lake somewhere, he opening the box, showing her the ring he had commissioned for her, he being sure to seek out the finest jewelry maker in town, knowing her discerning taste, and she saying she approved, the ring was lovely as the man is lovely, turning to him, kissing him, saying not today and not tomorrow, but there will come a day, I feel it, I believe it, something good is in our future?

YOU SHALL GO OUT WITH JOY
AND BE LED FORTH
WITH PEACE

I AM DEEPLY, DEEPLY AFRAID. Subtract seventeen years from my twenty-nine. I am twelve years old, standing beneath a starfruit tree, standing on an asphalt path lined with banyan trees, their roots extending from ground to sky to ground again and forming great pockets of wild, empty space in the center of their root-branches. Fifty feet behind me, the science laboratories where my chemistry teacher last week was too careless with sodium and set the ceiling tiles on fire. Fifty feet in front, the band room where the Sonshine Fellowship (Get it? Son, not sun! Like Jesus, the Son of God, the Light of the World who takes away our sins!) meets every Wednesday morning at 6:30 to pray and sing the happiest of songs all in major keys, except the songs borrowed from the Jews, which are in minor keys and which speed up as they go along and which, when played on acoustic guitars, are faintly reminiscent of sad country songs. And those happy songs make me happy, truly happy, for brief and ever briefer periods of time, but it's those Jewish songs—*You shall go out with joy and be led forth with peace. The mountains and the hills shall break forth before you . . .*—that really slay me, because there is something *earned* about that joy; it has come from a place of great pain.

The Jews, of course, are going to hell, but, as we students are constantly reminded, Jesus was a Jew, and the Jews are God's chosen people, and in fact we must keep the Jews around—this is the *real* reason why the Holocaust was so awful, because it was the work of the devil to destroy God's plan for the end of the world, which goes like this: Christ comes back in the clouds, this time on a white horse and bearing a sword, and bodily raptures all the dead in Him—a veritable zombie army—and the living Christians, too, the true ones (not, for instance, the Catholics, who follow a man, the pope; and not, for instance, the Episcopalians, who have placed a premium on the material needs of people rather than their spiritual needs—the Social Gospel, this is called—and so have slipped into heresy). The Christians, living and dead, taken bodily from the earth, leave a void of darkness. Remember, in the Book of Genesis, God promised to save the cities of Sodom and Gomorrah if Lot could find even one righteous man, but none could be found, so God rained fire upon the cities and they were destroyed. This, too, will be the fate of the earth, now that the righteous are gone. The Antichrist has already begun his seven-year reign. The clock is ticking. But—wait!—in that last hour 144,000 Jews finally accept Jesus as their personal Lord and Savior, many of them convinced and converted by two resurrected Jewish prophets. And then the Jews fight alongside the returning army of Christians at the battle of Armageddon, which takes place right in the heart of contemporary Palestine. God's chosen people, old and new, are finally reunited, and live together in the new heaven and the new earth—in the very bosom of God—forever.

But that's not why I am drawn to the Jews and their songs. It's not that I don't care about the rapture and Armageddon and the end of time. I am extremely anxious about it. For the last eight years—for as long, that is to say, as I have had memory—I have knelt in my bed, beside my window, at dusk, and watched the light show of sunset, looking for the crimson bloodstain in the sky that I've been told is a sign of His coming. I have memorized Scriptures—

If we confess our sins, He is faithful and just to forgive us our sins and cleanse us of all unrighteousness—and I live in fear of unforgiveness, of eternal hellfire, so I am constantly confessing my sins, an ongoing litany, a conversation, perhaps one-sided, between me and God, that consists for the most part of me trying to recount every sinful action (that part is easy) and every sinful thought (that part is hard). To look upon a woman with lust in your heart, for example, is the same as having slept with her. I am twelve years old. I am hard pressed to find a woman upon whom I will be able to gaze without feeling a twinge of lust in my heart. Puberty has come slow—my classmates, staring at my tiny naked body in the shower after Physical Education class, have made it quite clear that I am deficient in this area of puberty-arrival. But not entirely deficient. Sixth-period history: I am sitting behind Jenny Glass. Her blonde hair down to her shoulders, the shape of her hips, the sound of her voice humming softly, soft enough that Mr. Sanders can't hear, but loud enough that I can hear how fully rendered each of her notes, even at so soft a volume, such control . . . and then I'm wondering what it would be like to be married to her, and would we share a bed?, and what would *that* be like?, and I don't really know exactly what all that means—I mean, I know that there are parts, and that they fit, that kind of thing— but what I'm really thinking about is what it would be like to *kiss* Jenny Glass, to touch her hair as we kiss, feel it in the webbings of my fingers . . . and my body responds to these thoughts in its new way, and I lean forward a little in the desk, to obscure whatever it is that is happening, but of course it is at this moment that Mr. Sanders has had his say about the Battle of the Spanish Armada and is ready for me to have mine. "Kyle?" he says, and I say, "1588," and he says no, it's not enough to just know the date. You have to trace the sea routes on the four-color pulldown map, which he is right this moment pulling down over the chalkboard. Come on up, is what he says. And, right then, I do something that I've seen other people do but have never myself done. I say no, I'm not coming to the board to trace the sea routes on the four-color pulldown map. He asks why, and I say I'm not particularly interested in sea routes, that in fact I *prefer* dates and that I'm tired of being made to do things that I do not want to do. Mr. Sanders says if I don't walk directly to the blackboard and trace the sea routes that I will get a zero for the day's participation grade and that I'll be in grave danger of making him very angry. I consult my pants. My pants are saying no. Jenny Glass has turned around to look at me now, incredulous—the first opportunity, in fact, I've found to use that word, incredulous; I've been wanting to use it for a very long time, but now, employing it in my own mind, the word incredulous is nowhere near as sweet as I had thought it might be—and I briefly look at Jenny, trying to gauge her reaction to this turn of events, but I find that I am not able to look her in the eye. A slow, painful moment passes. Then, for the first time in my life, I deploy a coping skill that will soon become a lifelong crutch (and will also give those who wish for one a reason not to like me). I feign confidence. I say, "Mr. Sanders," and he says, "Yes?" and I borrow a line from a television comedian: "I'll take the zero."

What has this to do with the Jews, their songs? *You shall go out with joy and be led forth with peace*, sure, but first you will undergo great hardship. This from the prophet Isaiah, a truly mystifying figure, the greatest of the Hebrew prophets, come onto the scene at a pivotal point in Israel's history. Twenty years after Isaiah accepted his prophetic mantle, the Assyrians crushed the Northern Kingdom, and the better part of ten of the twelve tribes were taken into exile. (Twelve years old, and I know these things. They teach us these things at my school.) And not long after that, Jerusalem itself found the fearsome army of Sennacherib at its walls, and despite King Hezekiah's recent embrace of what Isaiah had called a "covenant of death" with a political faction that wanted Israel to be more like the Egyptians who had once held their ancestors as slaves— worship their idols, sleep with their women—Yahweh (YHWH; He whose name cannot be uttered on pain of death) delivered the city, and Sennacherib could only brag like a loser. *I shut Hezekiah up in his cage like a bird,* reads the famous inscription; not *Jerusalem is mine.*

Like all the prophets, Isaiah was both trouble and troubled, his destiny sealed when the seraphim cleansed his lips with a burning coal; and then, no doubt blistered and in great pain, he said, "Here am I, send me!" And then he wrote great, painful, angry poems of warning: *Your country is waste, your cities burnt with fire; Your land before your eyes strangers devour*—and—*the desert owl and hoot owl shall possess her, the screech owl and raven shall dwell in her*—and—*Take a harp, go about the city, O forgotten harlot; Pluck the strings skillfully, sing many songs, that they may remember you.*

I am twelve years old, standing beneath the starfruit tree, on the asphalt path, both hiding from and waiting for my daily beating. I know it is coming, because this morning the other science teacher, Mr. Guy, showed the filmstrip from *Answers in Genesis* about the fossil record—the dinosaur tracks with the human footprints embedded in them; the fragments of the Cro-Magnon man shown to be a hoax in a side-by-side comparison with a baboon skull; satellite imagery of the petrified remains of a massive seagoing vessel found lodged in the side of Mt. Ararat, in contemporary Turkey, where the Ark of Noah was said to have come to rest—and after class my head is so full of possibilities—a trip, perhaps, to Muslim Turkey, undercover, perhaps smuggling Bibles . . . perhaps even long hours under the sunlamp so I could pass for a Turk, following the example of the author of *Black Like Me* . . . and a daring climb with a Sherpa guide who would be proud when I bestowed upon him the Anglicized name of Henry . . . and a dig through snow and ice and earth to uncover, in person, what the satellites had already suggested: the Ark of Noah, proof beyond doubt, real archeological evidence of the worldwide flood that created the Grand Canyon, the Seven Continents, the washing-away of the Garden of Eden and, at last, rest for the angel who had been guarding it with his shining sword for all those many centuries . . . and also refutation of all the theories, the lies, that modern science has been serving up to support its religion of secular humanism—the Ice Age, Plate Tectonics, maybe Evolution itself— . . . my head so full of possibilities that I forget to go the long way to my math class, around the front of the gym that faces the administrative buildings, instead of the short way, around the back of the gym, near the locker rooms where Drew McKinnick and his boys lie in wait for me at this time every day. A careless, careless mistake that could have been so easily avoided, but I don't give one thought to it until I pass the pale green locker room door and forget to notice if it is cracked open or not, and then—WHACK!— McKinnick makes a weapon of the wooden door. It hits my arm with a velocity I could not begin to measure, and sends my body hard to the concrete, and—I have good reflexes; I'm used to this sort of thing—I manage to twist at the last moment, to wrench my body around so I land front-first rather than flat on my back, and hands-first rather than head-first—*bruise the hands, cut the hands; protect the head.* A teacher—good, Mr. Sanders, a good man—comes running from behind, and McKinnick is standing in front of my body—I see him up there, scratching his head, feigning concern, and feigning it in a manner that makes very clear his utter lack of concern— and Mr. Sanders says—he yells, really—"Why did you have to go and do that?" and McKinnick says, "I had no idea he was standing there," and Sanders says, "I doubt that sincerely," and McKinnick says, "On my honor, sir. I feel as bad about it as he does."

I know better. I know better than to say it. But I say, "No one feels as bad about it as I do." McKinnick can't help himself—it's only a moment; the slightest moment; the slightest of slightest moments— he smiles, flashes those dog teeth. In those teeth I see real pleasure, and it's not the first time, not by dozens. And then the smile is gone, and what's back is feigned regret. Sanders has his number, but who is Sanders? What can Sanders do? Sanders is already on thin ice for wiping boogers on the blackboard—to make us laugh; to make us feel better about ourselves; compassionate boogers—and before that, Sanders was already suspect, because Sanders moonlights as the school nightwatchman, because they don't pay him enough money, because he doesn't have a wife or children so he gets less than the other teachers, and sometimes he watches reruns of *Star Trek* on a black-and-white television at midnight in the principal's office, his feet up on the desk—he was caught once, and everyone knows—and another time he was caught falling asleep at two o'clock in the morning, and another time at five. They—*They*—say that Sanders jogs home at six-thirty every afternoon after coaching the junior varsity soccer team and sleeps until eleven-thirty, takes a quick shower, eats some Frosted Mini-Wheats, then humps it back to campus to nightwatch until dawn. That's Sanders, and what's Sanders next to McKinnick, whose father is the mayor of the village of Golfview, a veterinarian wealthier than God who paid for half the new football bleachers? And what's Sanders next to McKinnick, varsity linebacker in the eighth grade, second-string already, a mean two-twenty, putting hits on twelfth-grade running backs that they'll remember into their old age? McKinnick, who can crush a baseball, hit a three-hundred-fifty-foot shot to left-center. McKinnick, who could crush Sanders more ways than one.

The locker-room door cracks open. Jones, Dodd, Graves— McKinnick's boys. Sanders sees them. He says, "You boys get on to class." They pause for a minute. "Now," Sanders says, and they go, and McKinnick starts on his way, too, but Sanders says, "No, you wait," and I want to tell him . . . I want to tell him that what he is doing is a very bad idea. That it's a very bad idea for me. But I can't tell him. I can't say anything, because no matter what I say, it will make matters worse for me later. So I keep quiet. It's very hard to keep quiet.

"So what you're going to do right now, right at this very moment," Sanders is saying, "is apologize to Mr. Minor here."

McKinnick makes a sound in the back of his throat—the gathering of spit and phlegm—and then he turns his head and spits for

distance in the direction of the hedges that line the sidewalk outside the gym and locker rooms. The spit lands a few feet from the
hedges, and—I can't help myself—I say, "Airball," and then his eyes
flash like they can, the way I imagine the eyes of killers must flash in
the moment before they become killers—and, be advised, I believed,
then and now, McKinnick, given the right circumstances, fully capable of killing a man, or a boy, especially a boy, with his bare hands.

He looks right at me and smiles, and this time I detect nothing
but the utmost sincerity in that smile—and I know that the sincerity does not attach to the apology he is about to offer, but instead to
the retribution, the beating, that will follow—and he says, "Minor,
I'm truly sorry."

And Sanders says, "Good, then. It's settled. Now, both of you,
off to class."

I let him get a head start before I start walking. I know when
we turn the corner, mean Mrs. Tatham, the grammarian, will be
waiting outside her classroom door, watching, looking for an excuse
to jump down some poor kid's throat. God bless Mrs. Tatham.

McKinnick takes his head start. He rounds the corner, then I
do, and he is ahead of me, passing Mrs. Tatham, but then he slows
down. She is still watching, so he doesn't touch me, but when I get
within earshot he says—loud enough for me to hear, but soft enough
that she can't—"It's not settled"—and though I knew, now I *know*.

I am twelve years old, standing beneath the starfruit tree, pos-
sessing this terrible knowledge . . . and yet, and *yet*, above me are
starfruit, a great many, and I have been picking them for all the
years I have gone to this school, ever since I was four years old, and
I know how to pick one that is sweet enough but not overripe, and
not overly bitter, either. It is truly amazing to me that I am the only
person I know, student or teacher, who picks from this tree.

The fruit are green or yellow or brown, their color a measure
of their ripeness. I reach up and pick a yellow one, the five points of
its star just starting to turn brown. This is how I like them. Just a lit-

tle sweet, but still firm, not mushy. I bite into one of the points of the star and some juice runs down my face and down onto my hands and into the cuts and abrasions from where I caught myself on the concrete behind the pale green locker-room door after McKinnick hit me with it. There is citric acid in the juice, and when the acid touches the cuts and abrasions, it stings, and I make a fist involuntarily, and squeeze the starfruit I am holding, and squeeze more juice, more acid, into the wounds. *You shall go out with joy and be led forth with peace* is the song I am hearing in my head. *The mountains and the hills shall break forth before you*—all this from the naysayer, the prophet of doom who also wrote, *Your country is waste, your cities burnt with fire; Your land before your eyes strangers devour*—and the difference, you see, between Old Testament prophets like Isaiah and New Testament disciples is that the joy in these old Jewish writings always rises from the deepest of darkness, and there is no gloss on the darkness. No purpose for the darkness, except sometimes testing, sometimes judgment, sometimes spite, all this attributed often enough to God. No *all things work together for good to them who love God, to them who are called according to His righteousness.* No. All things do not work together for good. All things are in opposition, and the darkness more often overtakes the light than the light the darkness. The darkness is the darkness is the darkness.

And what would bring God joy? A final separation from sin. The destruction of the wicked. The destruction of the world.

And what would bring me joy? The destruction of Drew McKinnick.

I am twelve years old, standing beneath the starfruit tree, holding in my hand the most beautiful fruit any tree in the world has ever borne, and now softly humming the most beautiful, sad song I have ever heard—*You shall go out with joy and be led forth with peace*—and contemplating the destruction of Drew McKinnick.

There is the baseball bat. Maybe *his* baseball bat. I could carry it with me around the corner, make a show of showing it to Mrs.

Tatham, talk a little shop about the relationship between baseball bats and grammar. And wait. And when McKinnick rounded the corner, I could draw back that baseball bat and swing it at his head and explode his skull . . . no, watch it swell like a balloon, and then swing it again, and watch it pop, watch the splatter of gray matter and crimson blood stain the sidewalk, and then, in the moment before they wrestle me to the ground, kick that mouth with my black penny loafers, kick every last dog tooth from that mouth.

There is the baseball bat, but perhaps it is not practical. But then there is the gun. My grandpa has a loaded twelve-gauge shotgun mounted above his bed in his trailer. And a kid in my second-period study hall, Lee Paterson, has a book called *The Anarchist's Cookbook*. He says it is easy to make napalm. I told him once I'd like to napalm Drew McKinnick, and Paterson said it would be easy, that his skin would melt off, that he had tried this himself on a Barbie doll, and it had been only too easy.

"But what about a bomb?" Paterson had said.

"A bomb?"

"Two or three. Five or ten. Ten or twenty. Plant them all around. Blow the whole school down." He showed me a drawing he had made, a diagram of the school, and where the bombs would be placed. A few of them would go inside the air-conditioning units that lined the walls, because the component parts inside would become shrapnel and take out more people.

Paterson is small, smaller than me even, and I am the second smallest person in the whole secondary school. Some of the fourth and fifth graders are bigger than us. When he showed me the drawing, it scared me, first because I thought he might be serious, and second because I thought maybe I might be capable of doing it myself if I knew as much about chemistry and military strategy as he did. Looking at those diagrams, I thought I could maybe do it.

I am twelve years old, standing under the starfruit tree, eating a starfruit, thinking about blowing up the school, humming a

song written by the Jewish prophet Isaiah, holding all these contradictions in my head and not knowing that they are contradictions,
waiting for my beating; and then it arrives.

But not the way I think it will.

Because usually when McKinnick finds me to beat me, he
brings Jones and Dodd and Graves with him. They make a circle,
a loose circle at first, and they yell obscenities and push me from
one of them to another and sometimes push me down and kick
me and make me get back up so they can push me some more, but
then the circle tightens and McKinnick slaps my ears, hard, with
his open palm. First my ears ring, and then I lose most of my hearing and it doesn't come back for a couple of hours, and when it
does, it comes back with louder ringing and an awful headache.
Then Jones and Dodd and Graves hold me and slap the top of my
head and stick their spit-moistened fingers into my ears and nostrils while McKinnick stands over me and flicks the cartilage at the
tiptops of my ears with his fingers until the cartilage turns purple, and he keeps asking if I've had enough, and when I say yes,
he says, "No, you haven't," and when I say no, he says, "You need
to get some humility, boy," or, "Who do you think you're talking
to, boy," or, "Say *I'm a dirty nigger*. Say it. Say it." And then I say
it—"I'm a dirty nigger"—or—"I'm a queer, I'm a homo"—or—"I
fuck my mother"—or whatever other thing he wants me to say,
but even then it doesn't stop. Drew McKinnick knows how to hurt
a person a hundred ways and more, and there is nothing in the
world funnier, so far as I can tell, to Jones and Dodd and Graves
than to hold my arms while McKinnick lifts up my shirt and
grabs my nipples between his thumb and forefinger and tries to
turn them one-hundred-and-eighty degrees (this he calls a One-
Eighty), or to hold my arms and legs, to hold my whole body up in
the air while McKinnick slaps at my testicles like he did my ears,
with an open palm.

I'm waiting for that. I'm waiting for all that to happen.

But that's not what happens. What happens is I hear my
name—"Minor"—and I hear it behind me, from the direction of the
band room, where the Sonshine Fellowship meets to pray and sing.
I turn around. It's McKinnick, and he's alone. And the fact of this—
his aloneness—is more terrifying to me than anything I have ever
seen or heard or known or imagined in my entire life.

I am deeply, deeply afraid.

McKinnick starts running, takes off at a sprint, and I turn, too,
and start to run. But I am very slow. I get five steps, maybe, and he
tackles me from behind.

I fall face-first on the asphalt. I catch myself with my hands,
and my right hand goes through the starfruit on its way down and
rips fresh wounds into my hands, and those wounds are bathed in a
tiny new pool of citric acid.

McKinnick is on top of me. He mounts me from behind, starts
slapping my ears. "How's that?" he says, and slaps and slaps and
slaps and slaps, gets a rhythm going. He reaches into my pants and
grabs hold of my underwear with his hand and jerks the cotton into
my anus, and pulls, and pulls. I am already bleeding. I can feel the
warmth.

McKinnick says, "How's that? You like that? You feel it burn?
Burn, baby, burn!" He pulls my underwear up and down and from
side to side.

He says, "You know what? I could ass rape you right now and
no one would know. And if they found out, it's you would be the faggot, not me. You hear me, faggot? Are you listening?"

What does it feel like? It is the most helpless feeling in the world.
No one will come for me. If I try to tell on him—as I have done in the
past—no one will believe me. I am at his mercy, and I am not sure
he has any.

All I can do is go someplace else, to that band room, to
Wednesday mornings, 6:30 am, where I am singing—where we are
singing—the words of the prophet Isaiah: *You shall go out with joy*

and be led forth with peace. The mountains and the hills shall break forth before you. There will be shouts of joy, and all the trees of the fields will clap their hands, will clap their hands.

That, and this: I will grow up to become a person who will be able to make things like this not happen to other people. And I will tell this story. *This* story. I will make sure everyone knows.

And here I must interrupt the thoughts of my twelve-year-old self to tell you, reader, that I did *not* grow up to become a person who could keep things like this from happening to other people. And until this moment, this moment I am sharing with you, I did not grow up to tell this story. I tried, a few times, and less and less as years went by, to tell this story. But no friend ever wanted to hear this story. The past, they would say, is the past. Or: *That was a long time ago. Get over it.* Or: *Nobody likes victim stories.* And, most often, they would say nothing at all. They would just be very quiet—I could tell, always, from the looks on their faces, that I had made them very uncomfortable by sharing even the opening words of this confidence. I had revealed myself to be a very, very strange and disturbed individual.

I stopped trying to tell the story. I grew up, instead, to become a preacher. Briefly a preacher. Less than two years a preacher. And while I was a preacher I was befriended by a Palm Beach Gardens city worker, a meter reader named Tony Griffin, and it is important to know that Tony Griffin was black and that he was especially sensitive to racial issues, and that I was not—trained as I was, at this school, to not believe in any kind of legacy of racism in America, to believe that any talk of race was necessarily a crutch, an excuse used by black people unwilling to work hard, to pull themselves up by their bootstraps and all that. Tony and I had a falling out over this very issue. He was part of a small group of single people in their twenties and thirties who met at my house on Thursday nights to pray and read the Bible and play video games, mostly Madden Football '99, on my Sony PlayStation. And Tony was sure that the people in the group—all of them white but him—had turned against him because he was black. I was convinced that this charge was completely unfounded, and conceded that possibly the others were growing impatient because they disliked his habit of interrupting the PlayStation games to put kung fu movies in the VCR. So we broke off our friendship, Tony and I, over race and video games and kung fu movies. And then I quit being a preacher, decided to be a writer, lived in my car for a while.

I kept a cell phone, though, and one afternoon two years later it rang—I was near Orlando—and I saw Tony Griffin on the caller ID, and I answered and was glad to hear his voice until he said, "I'm calling because I have leukemia." And then I was making trips to West Palm Beach every couple of months to visit him in Hospice. And then we had another falling out. I didn't know that leukemia was a disease of the immune system, and I had a cold, and I came to visit, and I coughed as I walked through the door, and Tony threw a cup of red jello at my head and said, "Mother*fucke*r! You come in here with a *cold!*" I left the room as fast as I could and closed the door behind me, and I heard something else hit the door, and then: "I don't ever want to see your ass again until I'm *dead* and you're standing over my wooden box." I honored his wishes for a year, and then his niece called and said, "Come quick, he's got two days."

I walked into the room. He lay on the bed. His family was gathered there, waiting. He asked them to leave the room. He said, "No one will be straight with me. Am I going to die?"

I said, "I don't know."

He said, "Bring me a mirror."

I did, and he looked at himself for a long time, and then he said, "You ever see those pictures of the Ethiopian babies starving in the ditches?"

He bore a striking resemblance.

He said, "You see me, don't you?"

I nodded. I couldn't talk. What could I do? I crawled into the bed with him. He was naked beneath the hospital gown and he had shit himself and some of the shit got on my pants. I held him for a while, and then he said, "You were right about the kung fu movies."

And I said, "No, I wasn't. I wasn't right about anything."

This was death talk we were talking.

Then he said something extraordinary. He said, "I'm still praying for a miracle. I'm still believing for a miracle."

I did not want to tell him so I didn't tell him what I had learned, what life had taught me, which is there's no such thing as miracles. God doesn't probably answer our prayers.

After we said our goodbyes I left and knew he only had another day, probably, and it was not information I was equipped to handle. I hadn't cried since I was thirteen years old and received the last of my beatings from McKinnick. I had hardened myself so I wouldn't cry anymore, and then I couldn't undo it when I needed to undo it. So there I was, driving in my Chevy Corsica down Interstate 95, a little bit of Tony's shit still on my pants, just a little black stain, the little bit I couldn't get off with the hospital bathroom's hand soap and sink water. I was still trying to burn into memory what it was like to hold him and feel his flesh hanging like rags from the scaffolding of his bones, and to feel like if I held him too tightly I might break those bones and that it wouldn't take much at all. Not being able to cry made it all so much worse. The tightness in my chest was almost unbearable and I needed to somehow loosen the tightness, and even though the air conditioner was making the car uncomfortably cold, I felt a terrible heat in my chest and neck, and the veins in both temples were throbbing so hard I thought the vessels might burst. I pulled the car off on the side of the interstate, near a Jupiter neighborhood called The Heights where an ex-girlfriend still lived with her parents, their house a hundred feet or so from where I was sitting. I wanted to see her. I got out and scaled the six-foot chain-link fence separating neighborhood from interstate. My pants snagged on the fence and ripped a little, and I walked to her house and rang the doorbell. She wasn't there, but her mother answered the door and asked what was wrong and I told her that Tony was dying, and she said she was very sad and very sorry and wished she had time to talk about it but she had to be off to a birthday party.

And then I scaled that fence again, and ripped my pants some more, and that made me angry, ripping my pants. A state trooper a quarter mile away turned on his blue lights and raced toward me. I was standing beside the Chevy Corsica in ripped, shit-stained pants, my chest tighter, my neck hot, a shooting pain running down my left arm, watching the state trooper's blue lights parading like funhouse ghosts against the front of my shirt.

The trooper opened his door and stepped out, and then he looked at me, and I looked at him, and I saw that he was Drew McKinnick. I could feel the beating of my heart through my body. I could all but hear the ringing in my ears, and those old, familiar words: "You need to get some humility, boy." But then I could see that he *wasn't* Drew McKinnick. He only bore a striking resemblance. The same cold intensity in his eyes, same square jaw, same dog teeth.

A couple of years earlier, a state trooper had pulled my brother over on a dark road—he was still in high school and wore his hair long—and yanked him out of the car by the arm and threw him over the trunk and threw him around a little, asked him if he knew what happens to people who hit cops.

My officer, when he got a closer look at me, puffed out his chest, straightened to his full height. He asked what I was doing climbing the fence by the interstate. He was almost grinning. What passed between us was not unfamiliar. It was a flash of mutual recognition, the thing that two individuals of certain types immediately know about each other. Minor and McKinnick. I felt very small.

I told him I was having a hard time and I had stopped to see a friend. I said I knew I should not have climbed the fence. I said I would be glad to get back in my car and be on my way. I asked if he'd let me. I said I was very sorry. I was ready for him to throw me around, *knew* he would.

He waited a long time. He did not ask for my driver's license, and this troubled me. Whatever was going to happen between us was going to happen off the record. His nostrils flared when he breathed. He breathed hard. Each breath was like a calculated blow to the stomach. He put his hand on his holstered pistol. He looked into my eyes, measuring. I could not return his stare and shifted my focus to a fixed space beyond his shoulder, the white of the sky. "What happened to your pants?" he said, and I did not want to mention the fence. He seemed to find pleasure in my discomfort. He put his other hand on my shoulder and leaned over me so I had to look up again to meet his eyes. I told him I had ripped them on the fence. At that he grinned again, the predatory grin. His fingers dug into my shoulder. He said, "I don't want to see you on the side of this interstate again. That's a warning. I only give one. You understand?" I nodded. He sniffed the air, made a sour face. "Do yourself a favor and take a shower," he said. He gave my shoulder one last squeeze, then a little shove as he let go and walked back toward his patrol car and got in and waited for me to drive away.

I stepped into my car and drove away, and he followed me all the way to the Indiantown Road exit, and then I exited and he kept going north. I pulled into a service station, and then I began to sob. Present or not, Drew McKinnick had undone what he had undone. I could feel him in the presence of the cop. His joy at intimidation. Somehow I had made it possible. My ears were ringing though they had not been slapped. Somehow I still carried McKinnick around inside me. I cried for a long time, and if I said that I was crying for Tony dying, that would be true, but it would also be a very, very small portion of the truth. Mostly, I was crying for the twelve-year-old boy standing beneath the starfruit tree on the asphalt path and waiting for his beating.

When I had cried all I could cry, I started the car again. I dug through my cassette tapes and found one that Tony had given me, as a joke. It was Parliament/Funkadelic's Greatest Hits. We used to listen to that tape in the car all the time. I liked it more than he did.

I was listening to George Clinton go through the ministrations of "Atomic Dog"—*Why must I feel like that, why must I chase the cat?*—and then I was singing along, falsetto: *Nothin' but the dawg in me.*

The cell phone rang, and I knew it must be my brother—he was in Nashville auditioning for a six-month touring gig playing bass guitar for a well-known country singer—and I didn't even check the caller ID display. I answered and said, "Dr. Funkenstein here!"

And the voice on the other end was not my brother. It was Tony's niece. She said, "Kyle?"

I said, "Oh, oh, I'm so sorry, I didn't know."

"It's Tony," she said. "He's dead. He died a few minutes ago. I knew you'd want to know."

I didn't want to know. If this, dear reader, was a story like the kind I'd like to write, maybe there would have been a miracle. Most likely, Tony would die, but something else miraculous would happen. There would be a turn toward beauty that would reflect the joy-from-sadness in the prophet Isaiah's words, the comfort: *You shall go out with joy and be led forth with peace.*

But I can't do it. Not this time. At the funeral, when the other men who had been Tony's pastors gave their portion of the eulogy, their words were full of comfort and hope. They were able to assure his family that Tony was in a better place, that he was, in fact, in heaven, with Jesus and the angels, held close to the bosom of God. But when it was my turn, I had no comfort or hope left to give. All I could say was that I loved Tony, and that he loved me, and that he was a stubborn and intractable person, and that I was, too, and that I believed, truly, that Tony had found his greatest joy in watching kung fu movies. That was all I could say. And when I was done,

I stepped down from the only pulpit from which I had ever preached a sermon, and I walked past the altar, and down the steps, and down the aisle, and through the back doors of the church, and I have not been back since.

THE TRUTH AND
ALL ITS UGLY

I.

THE YEAR MY BOY DANNY TURNED SIX, my wife Penny and me took him down to Lexington and got him good and scanned because that's what everybody was doing back then, and, like they say, better safe than sorry.

He was a good boy and never got out of hand until he was seventeen years old and we got out of hand together. Around this same time Penny kept saying she was going to leave and stay with her sister in town. She said it enough that we stopped believing her, but the last time she said it, she did it. I remember the day and the hour. Friday, September 17, 2024. Quarter after five in the afternoon, because that's what time her grandmother's grandfather clock stopped when I kicked it over.

Danny heard all the yelling, and he came running downstairs and saw her standing there with her two suitcases and looked at me like I ought to do something. "Goddamn it, I'm not going to stop her," I said.

"It's your fault she's going," he said.

Penny hauled off and slapped his mouth. "I didn't raise you to talk to your father that way," she said, and at that moment I was of

two minds, one of them swelled up with pride at the way she didn't
let him mouth off to me.

It's the other one that won out. I reached back and gave her
what she had coming for a long time now. I didn't knock her down,
but I put one tooth through her lip, hit her just hard enough so she
would come back to us when she was calmed down.

She didn't come back, though, and she didn't go stay with her
sister, who claimed not even to know where she was. One week, two,
then on a Saturday me and Danny had enough. We hauled Penny's
mother's pink-painted upright piano out the front door and onto the
porch and then we pushed it off and picked up our axes from by the
wood pile and jumped down on it. "You got to be careful, Danny," I
said. "There's a tension on those strings that'll cut you up bad you
hit them wrong."

It was pure joy, watching him lift that axe and drive it into that
piano. Up until then his head was always in books or that damn
computer. Dead trees, I'd tell him, got not one thing on milkweed
and sumac, horsemint and sweet William. But now I wasn't so sure,
and now he'd caught on. "It's what you do with the dead trees," he
said, like he was reading my mind.

I don't know what came over us after that, and it's not enough
to blame it on our getting into the whiskey, which we did plenty.
Penny had a old collection of Precious Moments figurines handed
down from her own mama and grandmom. Children at a picnic, or
playing the accordion to a bunch of birds, or hands folded in prayer,
and nearly every little boy or girl wearing a bonnet. At first Danny
said we ought to shoot at them—we had everything from assault
rifles to a old Civil War service revolver that I'd be afraid to try firing—but then one Tuesday morning—by now it was November,
and the old dog pens were near snowed under—he found some of
the yellowjackets I had caught in glass Mason jars and forgot about.
He found them dead in there and I saw him looking at them and he
saw me watching but didn't say anything, just went upstairs and

came down with my old orange tacklebox, which was where Penny kept her scrapbooking things.

"You gonna scrapbook those yellowjackets, buddy bear?" I said.

He said his plan was to shellac them. He couldn't near do it right, and I said, "Here, let me show you how," and showed him how to thin the shellac with turpentine and dab it on soft with the paintbrush bristles, which was something I knew from when things were better with Penny and I'd help her with her scrapbooks just so we could sit with our legs touching for a while.

He got good at it fast, and then we caught more yellowjackets and did what Danny had in mind all along, which was shellac them stiff, wings out like they were ready to fly, and set them on the Precious Moments figurines in a swarm.

After a while that stopped being fun, and it kind of took the shock away when every Precious Moment in the house was swarmed like that, plus we were running out of yellowjackets. "We got to get more minimal," Danny said, and I could see what he meant. It's like when I served my country in the African wars. You get to see enough dead bodies and after a while you get used to seeing them, and then you see another and it don't mean one thing to you. But you run into one little live black girl with a open chickenwire wound up and down her face and maybe three flies in her cut-up eye, that gets to you.

So after that, we got strategic. We'd put three yellowjackets right by a brown marbly eye, eye to eye. Or one, stinger first.

Nobody but us had got to see what we had done to the Precious Moments until a few days later when Benny Gil, our postman, came by with the junk mail, and Danny saw him and invited him in for a glass of water, and he saw what it was we were doing with the wasps, and he said, "Son, that's sick," but he was smiling when he said it, and it was then I knew he was a person who could be trusted. Up until then, he'd always been asking about my methadone, which

I got regular from the pharmacy at St. Claire's Hospital in town, on account of my back pain. He wanted to get some off me because he could trade it for other things he wanted.

This day I asked him, "Why is it nobody writes letters anymore?"

"It's a general lack of literacy," he said, and we started laughing because everybody knew that wasn't why.

"It's the government," Danny said, but he was just repeating what he always heard me say, and I wished he wouldn't get so serious in front of Benny Gil.

"They're spying," Benny Gil said, "listening in on us right now," but he wasn't serious.

"Best be careful," I said, because now was a time to keep it light. "Benny Gil here is on the government teat."

Benny Gil took a sip of his water and smiled some more. "That one," he said, "and maybe a couple two or three others."

Danny caught on. "It's you we saw across the creek there, in the tall grass."

"I been watching," Benny Gil said. He leaned back in the wooden chair, put all his weight on the back two legs. I could see by the look on Danny's face he was still thinking about how Penny would say not to lean back like that because it could put another divot in the wood floor, which was the kind of not important thing Penny was always worried about. There was a thousand or more divots in the wood floor, and by now another one just added a little extra character.

Benny Gil leaned forward again, put his elbows on his knees so his face was closer to mine. "I know where Penny can be found," he said.

Danny's ears perked up at that.

"She wants to be found," I said, "and I don't care to find her."

"Irregardless," Benny Gil said.

"Where is she?" Danny said, and I shot him a look.

"Maybe," Benny Gil said, "me and your dad ought to go out back and have a smoke."

Danny watched us through the window, and I wonder what it is he was thinking and wonder to this day whether whatever it was he thought had anything to do with what he did later. Surely he saw something changing hands between me and Benny Gil, and he must have seen us shaking hands, too.

What he didn't hear was Benny Gil saying, "God didn't invent thirteen-digit zip codes for nothing," or me saying, "How many?" or him saying, "Sixteen," or me talking him down to six. Six, I could spare, by careful rationing, and by grinding the white pills into white powder with my pocketknife, and snorting them instead of swallowing, which meant I could stretch out the supply until it was time for a new scrip.

Danny didn't hear any of it, but maybe he knew something of it, because after Benny Gil left, he said, "You get to hurting again, I know somebody who can get you what you need."

"Who?"

"Ben Holbrook," he said.

"That's the case," I said, "I don't want to hear of you talking to Ben Holbrook ever again."

I meant it when I said it, but the problem was the methadone got better after I started grinding it up, and once I knew how much better it could get, I had a harder time rationing it, and ran out a week early.

Believe me when I say I know a thing or two about pain. I was wounded twice in Liberia, and got radiation poisoning from the Arabs in Yemen. Once in Minnesota I split a fourteen-point buck in half on a old fossil fuel motorcycle and broke nearly every bone in my body and knocked one eye crooked, and it stayed that way until I could afford to get it fixed. But, son, you don't know pain until you get what I got, which is a repetitive stress injury in my back from solar panel installations up there on roofs in the heat or the cold. So when the methadone ran out, I forgot about what I said before, and told Danny maybe if he knew somebody he ought to give him a call.

Ben Holbrook was a skinny son of a gun, no more than maybe eighteen years old, pimple-faced, head shaved bald so you could see its lumps. Money was not a problem for us. Benny Gil wasn't the only one on the government teat, he just had to work for his. Still, I didn't like the way this bald zitty kid came into our house thinking he was the only one who could set prices in America.

"Who do you think you are," I said, "Federal Reserve Chairman Dean Karlan?"

He was cool as a cucumber. "Supply and demand," he said, "is the law of the land in Kentucky, U.S.A."

Much as I didn't like it, I knew he was right, and I paid what he asked, which was considerable, and he handed over three brown-orange plastic bottles, which was supply enough for my demand and then some.

Soon as Ben Holbrook left, I went into the bathroom with my pocketknife and dropped two tablets on the sink counter and chopped them to powder and made a line. Then I put my nose low to the Formica and closed off my right nostril with a finger and snorted the line through my left.

I must have left the door open a crack, because I saw Danny there, just outside, watching. He knew it was a thing I was doing, but I don't think he ever saw me do it before.

I knew good and well that wasn't the type of thing I wanted him to see. Any other time I would have thrown a shoe at him if I caught him spying like that. But when you take your medicine through your nose, it hits your bloodstream fast and hard. That's why you take it that way. So my first thought was to throw a shoe, but before that first thought was even gone the juice hit my bloodstream, and there was my boy, his eyes looking at mine through the crack in the bathroom door, and if I ever loved him I loved him more in that now than in any ever, and right alongside that first thought was the second, which came out my mouth the same time it came into my head, even though I knew it was wrong as I thought it and said it. "Boy," I said. "Come on in here and try a line."

Some things you see like from outside yourself and from above, and that's how I see what happened next. Right there, below, there's big old me, and there's my boy Danny, and I'm coming around behind him, putting my arms around him like I did when I showed him how to line up a cue stick at Jack's Tavern or sink a putt at the Gooney Golf, and he's got the open pocketknife in his hand, and I've got his hand in my hand, pushing down on it, showing him how to crush without wasting anything, how to corral the powder, how a good line is made. That's me, leaning down, pantomiming to show him how. That's him, fast learner, nose to the counter, finger to nostril. There's the line, gone up like the rapture. Danny, standing up too fast because he don't know any better, and the trickle of blood down his lip and chin, and me, tilting his head back, cradling it in the crook of my arm, putting the old Boy Scout press on his nose with a wad of toilet paper, saying, "Hold still now, baby boy," and his eyes bright, and his cheeks flushed, and his voice like from a hundred miles away saying, "Lord, have mercy," then, "Weird," and us lying back, then, on the cold tile, his shoulder blades resting on my chest, both of us waiting for the hit to pass so we could take another.

The days and nights started going by fast after that, and sometimes there was no cause to tell one from the other. One morning or afternoon or midnight, for all I know, I went into my room and found Danny half-naked underneath the bed I shared for all those years with Penny, and when I asked him what he was doing under there, he said, "She's been after us all this time," and I said, "Who?" and he said, "Her," and hauled out a stash of scented candles his mother must have left under there, cinnamon and jasmine and persimmon-lemon.

At first I thought he was talking crazy, but then he pulled himself out from under the bed and walked real close and put the purple jasmine one under his eye and struck a blue tip match and lit the wick, and soon as it started to burn his eye went all bloodshot and swelled up. Even still, I wanted to take up her case.

"How was she to know?" I said, but he was looking at me hard. "Turn around," he said, "and look in that mirror." And sure enough, my eye was tearing up and swelling and all the blood vessels were turning red.

"Benny Gil," he said, "told you where she is."

"That's not strictly true," I said, except it was.

"The general area, then," he said.

"The general neck of the woods," I said.

He went into me and Penny's bathroom, then, and for some reason, even though we had being doing it together, I couldn't go in there just then and do it with him. I could hear him, though, and then I heard a few more sounds I knew but hadn't expected to hear, which were the sounds of him loading my old Browning 9mm, which I kept under the sink in case of emergencies. When I heard that, I got scared, because for a while now I had been feeling, like I said before, like things were getting out of hand, but now, him stepping out of the bathroom, hand around the grip of that nine, I had the kind of proof that makes it so you can't look the other way anymore.

"Killing," I said, "isn't a kind of thing you can take back."

"I don't mean to kill her," he said. "I just mean to scare her a little."

That was more sensible talk than the talk I had been expecting from him, but still not altogether sensible. He was angry, I knew, after finding those candles, and I can't say I wasn't angry, either, but when you're young and full of piss and vinegar, caution is not a thing you take to naturally, and, besides, neither one of us was going through life in any kind of measured way at that particular point.

"I'm not saying she don't deserve a little scaring," I said. "When the time comes you'll see me front and center, taking the pleasure you and me both deserve after everything. But what I'm saying is that the time isn't come. Not yet."

"Look around," Danny said, and all around us was eighteen kinds of mess, some we'd made, and some that had just kind of grown while we weren't paying attention. "Sheila," he said, which was the name of a dog we'd had once who had abandoned her young before it was time, and all five of them had died, and who I had taken out back and shot because there wasn't one good thing about a dog who would go and do that.

"We're grown," I told him.

"Not me," he said.

There wasn't much I could say to that, because it was true, but I got him to hand over the Browning, and then he went upstairs and didn't come down for the rest of the night, and I figured he'd be down when he got hungry enough.

I went into the kitchen and made some pancakes and made some extra and wrapped them in foil and put them in the refrigerator so he could have them later. Then I put some butter and maple syrup over mine and ate them and drank some milk and fell asleep in front of a old Wesley Snipes movie and figured when I woke up I'd see if he didn't want to put on his boots and go out into the Daniel Boone National Forest and hike for a while and get cleared out the way the cold air will do you.

When I woke up, though, the car was gone, and the extension cord for the battery charger was running from the living room out the front door, and I followed it on out to the side of the house where we parked the car, which was sure enough gone, and with juice enough to go to Lexington and back probably. That's when panic kicked in, and I ran back into the house, toward me and Penny's bathroom, knowing the Browning was going to be gone, but hoping it wasn't, and when I got there and didn't find it where it should have been, I figured there wasn't any way I was going to see Penny alive again, but I was wrong.

2.

It was Penny who found him. It took some time, but after a while
the authorities pieced together what had happened. Around six
in the evening, they said, must have been the time I fell asleep.
When the house got quiet enough, Danny went out to the shed and
brought in the long extension cord and ran it to the car battery.
While it was charging he loaded up three assault rifles, including
the Kalashnikov 3000, the one made to look like a AK-47 but with
the guts of a MicroKal, laser gun and flamethrower and all. He took
the Browning, too, and my bowie knife, and his old play camo war
paint, and a cache of armor-piercing bullets, although he never did
use any of it except the 9mm. Then he sat down and ate the pancakes I had made, and washed off the plate and knife and fork he
had used to eat them, and left them out to air dry.

By time he got to Benny Gil's house, he had worked himself
up into something cold enough that Benny Gil didn't argue, didn't
even need to be shown knife or gun to know it was in his best inter-
est to give up Penny's location and get Danny on his way. I don't
know what that means, exactly, except to say that Benny Gil is not
a person I've ever known or heard of to be afraid of anyone or
anything.

What Benny Gil told Danny was that Penny was staying with
her sister's husband's nephew Kelly, a bookish boy we never knew
well because he never came around to family things, probably
because he, or more likely his mother, thought he was better than
us, from what they call a more refined stock.

Kelly was, by then, well-to-do, UK law degree in hand, spe-
cialty in horse law. He even had a office at Keeneland and another
at Churchill Downs, and if he thought as highly of himself as
he seemed to every year on the television, sitting there next to
some half-dead Derby owner who needed a oxygen tank just to

breathe, sipping a mint julep, then I'm sure him and Penny made a fine pair.

There's no way to know it now, but my guess is that Danny, when he heard of it, came to the same idea I did when I first heard of it, which was something not right was happening between Penny and that boy, but I put it out of my head at the time because it was too horrible a thing to look at directly.

At any rate, what happened next is the part of the story that got out into the world. Danny drove east on Interstate 64, stopped at the Sonicburger in Mt. Sterling and ordered and ate a egg sandwich, then headed toward the big expensive stone houses by the airport, where Penny and Kelly was shacked up.

When he got there, he rang the doorbell three times—that's what Kelly's security company came up with later—and nobody was home, and I guess he didn't want to wait, and I guess he knew well enough what ended up being true, which was that there was something worse for a mother than to be killed by her son.

At the funeral, the preacher and everyone else said that wasn't the case, that Danny was sick in the head and that these things happen in the brain, something trips or snaps or misfires, and then somebody is doing something they wouldn't do if they were themself. But I think that's the kind of thing people say when what they want to do is make themselves feel better instead of look straight ahead at the truth and all its ugly. Because what I think and pretty near to know happened goes like this:

When he got there, he rang that doorbell three times, and nobody was home, and he got to thinking, and what he was thinking about was clear enough to him, and what he was thinking was that he had come all this way to hurt his mother, and his stomach was full from that egg sandwich, and that Browning 9mm was in his hand, and what if instead of killing her and just hurting her that one time, what if instead he did himself right there where she would have to come home and find him, and wouldn't that be something she would have to live with, and go on living and living and living? And wouldn't that be the way to hurt her again and again, the way she had hurt him and us by running off?

So that's what he did. He sat down in front of Kelly's front door, and put the muzzle to his right temple, and turned his head so his left temple was to the door, and when Penny came home that night, what she found was the worst thing you can ever find, and when I heard about it, I couldn't hate her the way I wanted to anymore.

At the funeral, they sat us both on the front row, but far apart from each other, with a bunch of her brothers and other male relatives between us so I would know clear as daylight that I was meant to stay away from her. But before the service got started, the preacher came over and asked if there were things each of us needed to say to the deceased, and we both said yes, but for me it wasn't because I had anything to say to Danny. He was dead and gone and wherever it is he ended up, and that was hard enough to bear without making a show of telling him something he wasn't ever going to hear. It was Penny I wanted to say some things to, and I thought maybe up there next to Danny she might in that moment have ears to hear them.

Her brothers didn't leave the room when the preacher asked, but they did go stand in the back and give what they must have thought was a respectful distance. Me and Penny went and knelt beside the casket, her near his head and me near the middle, maybe three feet separating us. She bowed her head to pray silently, and I did, too, although I didn't right then have any words to say, and then she said some things to Danny too personal for me to repeat, although I don't think it would be wrong to say that the things she said, if they were true, moved me in a way I didn't think I could be moved by her.

When she was done, she looked over at me. It seemed like she was able to keep from crying all that time until she looked into my eyes, and I was reminded that it was our looking into each other's eyes that was happening while we were about the business of getting him made in the first place, and maybe that's what she saw that finally broke her down when she looked over at me. Maybe that, and all the years we had together, the three of us, and how there wasn't anyone else in the world who knew what those years were, and how there wouldn't ever be anyone else again.

It was right then, though I didn't say anything at the time because it didn't seem like the right time, that I decided I couldn't live in a world where Penny would go on being as unhappy as she had been made to be.

First thing the next morning I went down to Lexington again and went to the place where we had taken Danny to get scanned when he was six years old. It was gone, boarded up, the part of town where it had been now all but forgotten by people in business to make money. The only place in the storefront where the lights were still on was the WIC food stamp place, and I went inside and was told where to go on the Loop, to a part of town I remembered as Lexington Green but which was now called Stonewall.

The business had changed its name too, was now called Livelong, and occupied a building the size of a city block. The woman at the front desk said my number was A83, gave me a smart-pad to fill in and told me to take a seat.

By time they called my name I had run my fingerprint and verified all my information and watched the screen that said the scan we had got was old technology, and while the guarantee we had bought was still good, the Danny we would get would eventually wear out, but would not age the way the ones they could make now could. We'd get him six years old, and six years old he would stay.

They made me meet with a kid in a suit and tie, and all he said was the same thing I had heard from the smartpad. He was looking at me funny, and I said, "All I want to get is the service I paid for eleven years ago, near to the day," and he lowered his head for just a moment, like he was ashamed, and then he said, "You're entitled to it, and we'll give it to you if you want, but what you need to know is sometimes what you want isn't the same as the thing we can give you."

Even though he was a kid, what he was saying was true, and I knew it then, and it made me want to pound the sense out of him, and even so I wanted what I wanted.

I walked out of that Stonewall storefront that afternoon holding the warm flesh hand of a thing that moved and talked and looked for the life of me just like Danny did at six years old, and it was nearly unbearable, at first, to touch him or hear him say, "Now we're going for ice cream, Daddy?" and to remember the bargain we had made with Danny the day we took him to get him scanned. *You be good through this,* we'd told him, *we'll take you to get whatever kind of ice cream you want.*

So I said, "Sure, buddy bear," and I took him up the road to the Baskin Robbins, and he ordered what Danny always ordered, which was Rocky Road with green and only green M&M's sprinkled over top, and we got a high table for two, and I sat and watched him chew exactly the way he used to chew, and lick the spoon exactly the way he used to lick the spoon. He said, "Can we split a Coke, Dad?" and I said sure, and went up to the counter and ordered a large Coke, and when I forgot to get an extra straw, I regretted it the way I used to regret it, because he chewed the straw down to where you could hardly get any Coke out of it.

After that he wanted to go walk the old stone wall like we always did when we came to Lexington, so I took him down there and parked the car and got him out and hoisted him up on the wall, and held his hand to steady him as he walked on top of it, and he said, "Tell me about the slaves, Daddy," so I did what I used to do and told him about how all the black people in Kentucky used to belong to the white people, and how this very wall he was walking on had been made by their hands, one stone at a time, and the mortar mixed with probably some of their sweat and maybe some of their blood, too, still in it, and how even with all that Kentucky fought for the Union and could well have been the difference in that war. While I was saying it, I was remembering how I used to believe things like that, and the feelings that used to rise up in my chest when I said them, feelings of pride and certainty, and warm feelings toward my people I had come from. These were stories my own dad and granddad used to tell me and which I was now passing along to my own son, and this little Danny, walking along that wall, holding my hand, said the same thing the other little Danny had said in a moment a whole lot like this one but which couldn't have been, if you think about it, any more different if it was happening on the other side of the world. He said, "It wasn't right, was it, for people to keep other people to do their work for them? How did anybody ever think it was right?"

And I said the same thing I said then, which was, "People don't always do what's right, son, but you and me get the privilege of making our own choices, and we have to make good choices. That's what makes a person good, is the choices you make."

Right then is when we went off the script. Could be that something was wrong with his making, or could be that I wasn't leading him right, but right at that moment, he took a wrong step and fell. He didn't fall off the wall altogether, but he caught his shoe on a stone that was sticking up at a bad angle, and when he fell, he caught his arm on another stone, and it cut deep into his skin, and when he tried to stand up, he pulled away and didn't seem aware that his skin was caught on that rock. I guess they don't build those things in such a way that they feel pain the same way you and me do, because as he stood up, the skin of his arm began to pull away from what was underneath, which wasn't bone or sinew, but cold lightweight metal, what I now know they call the endoskeleton, and what began to drain from him warm wasn't his own blood, but somebody else's, and the reason it was in there wasn't to keep him alive, but just to keep his skin warm and pink, just to make him look and feel like someone alive.

"Danny," I said. He must have heard the alarm in my voice, and I could tell it scared him. He looked down and saw his metal arm, the skin hanging off it, and the blood pouring out in a way that wasn't natural, and then he gave me a look that sank my soul, and I realized what I should have realized before I signed what I signed, which was that I had got them to make a boy out of something that wasn't a boy. All that was in his head was all that was in Danny's head a long time ago, back when Danny was himself someone different than who he became later, and it wasn't his fault. He didn't know what he was, and the sight of it was more than he could handle.

His lip began, then, to tremble, in the way Danny's did when he needed comforting, and I lifted him down off that stone wall and took him in my arms and held him and comforted him, and then, in the car, I stretched the skin back to where it had been, and took Penny's old emergency button-sewing kit out of the glove compartment and took needle and thread to it and got him to where none of the metal was showing. I didn't take him to Penny's like I had planned.

He was real quiet all the way home. He just stared straight ahead and didn't look at his arm and didn't look at me. Near Winchester I asked him if he wanted to hear some music, and he said all right, but we couldn't find anything good on the radio. "How about the football game?" I said, and he said all right again, and we found the Tennessee Titans and the Dallas Cowboys, and I made a show of cheering for the Titans the way we always had, but when he said, "How come all their names are different?" I didn't have a good answer, and after that I asked if he wouldn't mind just a little quiet, and he said he wouldn't mind, and I leaned back his seat and said, "Why don't you just close your eyes and rest awhile? It's been a long day and I bet you're tired."

He did. He closed his eyes then, and after some time had passed and I thought he was asleep, I stroked his hair with my free hand and made some kind of mothering sounds.

It was dark when we got to the house. I parked the car by the bedroom window, then went around to his side and picked him up like I was going to carry him sleeping to bed. I held him there in the dark for a little while and thought about that, carrying him up to bed, laying him there, laying his head on the pillow, pulling the covers up around his shoulders, tucking him in. It would have been the easiest thing to do, and it was the thing I wanted to do, but then I got to thinking about Penny, and sooner or later, I knew, she would have to be brought in on this, and even though I thought I had done it for her, I could see now that I had really done it for me, like maybe if I showed up with this little Danny she would come back home and the three of us could have another go of it.

But already this little Danny was wearing out. I could feel it in his skin. He wasn't warm like he was when I had picked him up, I guess because the blood had run out of him on the stone wall. He was breathing, but he was cold, and a little too heavy compared to what I remembered. There wasn't any future for him, either. I got to thinking about how if I put him in school, everyone would get bigger than him fast, and it would get worse every year, the distance between who he was and who his friends were becoming.

He was stirring a little, so I put his head on my shoulder, the way I used to do, and patted his back until his breathing told me he was asleep again. Then I went around to the front of the house and reached up to the porch and took down my axe from the wood pile and went off into the woods, down the path I had mowed with my riding mower a few weeks back, and which was already starting to come up enough that I had to watch my step.

I kept walking, him on my shoulder, axe in my free hand, until I reached the clearing. Then, careful not to wake him, I unbuttoned my jacket and got it out from under him and took it off and laid it on the ground. Then I laid him down on it and made sure he was still sleeping. Then I lifted up the axe and aimed it for the joint where his head met his neck and brought it down. In the split second right before blade struck skin, I saw his eyes open, and they were wide, and what I saw in them was not fear but instead some kind of wonder, and then, fast as it had come, it was gone, and all I could tell myself, over and over, was *It's not Danny. It's not Danny.*

GLOSSOLALIA

"ARE YOU INTERESTED IN ME BECAUSE I'm a girl or because I love Jesus?"

"I am interested in you because I like you."

"But if I didn't love Jesus, would you still be interested in me?"

"I would like to think that I would be interested in you no matter what."

"But if I didn't love Jesus, I don't think I would be the same person."

"If you didn't love Jesus, I think in some ways you would be the same person."

"But I wouldn't see the world the same way, I wouldn't read the same things, I wouldn't make the same choices, I wouldn't be around the same people."

"But I think you would still like a lot of the same things. You would still be a ski instructor in the winter. You would still spend the summer here on the beach. You would still run. You would still bodysurf. You would still be physically very beautiful. You still would be a person who cares about other people, and you still, probably, would have taught me to bodyboard."

"But I used to be a person who didn't love Jesus. I used to make different choices. Like when I was a freshman in college, there was this older guy, and he used to come into my room and sleep in my bed and he knew how to do things with his hands and his mouth. He knew how to make me feel things."

"You didn't have sex with him even though you didn't yet love Jesus."

"I didn't have sex with him because I had an idea of Jesus, but I didn't yet really know Jesus. I thought I did, but I didn't."

"But you prayed to Jesus, didn't you?"

"I did pray to Jesus, but not in tongues."

"When did you start to pray in tongues?"

"When I was filled up with the Holy Spirit."

"Is that when you stopped messing around with this guy?"

"No. It was later. There were other guys. In Madrid, this one guy took me to an R.E.M. concert."

"Did it make you feel dirty to mess around with him?"

"No. It made me feel good. But I still felt empty inside."

"How did you learn how to pray in tongues?"

"I prayed to be filled up with the Holy Spirit, and then I was given the gift."

"Can you do it on command?"

"I can do it anytime, if that's what you mean."

"Can I hear you do it?"

"Would you like to pray with me?"

"Will you do it if I pray with you?"

"When I pray I do it. It comes naturally."

"How do you know what it is you are saying if you are speaking a language you don't know?"

"I don't know what I am saying. It is my spirit that knows what I am saying. My spirit is communing directly with God's spirit. I can't explain it, but I can feel it, like this energy pulsing through me."

"If I held your hand, could I feel the energy, too?"

"I feel like you are being glib."

"I am not being glib. I just feel like this is something I don't understand but I really do want to understand. I want to be a person who is open-minded to new experiences."

"Take my hand. Here. Take my other hand. Let's pray."

•

"What did you think just now, when I was speaking in tongues?"

"I thought a lot of the sounds were repeated and there were a lot of consonant clusters. I heard maybe some sounds that sounded like German and some sounds that sounded like Hebrew or Arabic maybe. There were also a lot of sounds that you don't make when you speak in English, like rolling your R's and flattening out your O sounds."

"That's true. I have noticed those things, too."

"Do you ever try to think about recording what you say when you say it? Like, maybe you could do some code-breaking and make a dictionary."

"Again, I feel like maybe you are being glib."

"Hear me out. I'm being serious. The idea is you are speaking a language that people don't speak on earth, except people who speak the language of angels. So consequently, if you follow the logic, it's a real language. So wouldn't it have the things a real language has, like grammar and syntax and vocabulary? And if that's so, couldn't you study it just like you could study any other language?"

"That's movie stuff. That's like something starring Patricia Arquette."

"Why not, though? There's people who do this for a living. They go over to Papua New Guinea or wherever, and they spend time around a language, and then they reconstruct it, even though when they first get there they don't know the first thing about it."

"That's missing the whole point."

"Why?"

"Because if you knew the language, then the purity of the communication would be lost. You'd start crafting all the words instead of the spirit that indwells in you crafting the words."

"But—and here I'm not being glib, I'm just trying to understand—don't you want to know what it is you are speaking to Jesus or the angels or whatever?"

"You don't pray to angels."

"But it's an angel language, right?"

"The idea is that you're not in control. You're giving yourself over to it."

"Is that why you jerk your body to the left when you pray in tongues?"

"That's a manifestation."

"Why do you do it?"

"I don't do it. It comes over me when I give myself over to the Spirit."

"Does it happen to everyone who speaks in tongues?"

"Some people fall down like they are dead."

"That's slain in the Spirit."

"Right. Some people fall into fits of laughter. Some people bark like dogs, but not too many people. I don't want to judge, but I think sometimes when that happens a lot it can be for show. But I don't know."

"That's something that worries me. It's a little bit frightening, don't you think, like on TV, when a lot of people are doing it all around, and there's this ungodly cacophony?"

"That's the fear of the Lord you're feeling."

"How can you be sure?"

"How can you be sure of anything? You know. I know. I know that I know that I know."

"Here this stuff is at odds with logic, maybe, I think."

"I think that's a wrong way to think about it, but tell me what you're thinking."

"I took this philosophy class. Dr. Willard Reed. He was talking about the distinction between belief and knowledge. He said knowledge is problematic. You can't really know stuff that isn't somehow verifiable. Like you didn't see it with your own eyes or experience it yourself or there hasn't been some kind of consensus among the people who study the thing. And even then there's problems. How do you know you aren't fooling yourself? Or how do you know the consensus might not be wrong. Like the consensus used to be that the earth was flat. And on top of that, how do you know that the universe didn't just begin two seconds ago. After a while, everything starts to be belief."

"I don't guess it matters much which is which, then, if it's all so slippery."

"I don't guess it does."

"But what kind of way is that to live? Walking around not being sure of anything. Everything tentative. No place for boldness. No place for meaning. Wouldn't that just throw you into some kind of paralytic feedback loop or something? Wouldn't you just be staring at your navel forever?"

"Not necessarily, but I don't know. You just described a lot of the way I think a lot of the time."

"That's why you have to let go control. That's what praying in the Spirit is. You're letting go that control and giving yourself over to your creator. It's an act of faith in the unseen. Although, I have to tell you, there are things I have seen."

"What kinds of things?"

"Visions. Gold dust."

"Gold dust?"

"There have been meetings where the Spirit of God has come down and the manifestation was gold dust that began to appear on everyone's shoulders."

"Manifestations, like the jerking to the left."

"I'm not going to say anymore if you're going to mock everything."

"Honestly, I'm not mocking. I really want to know. Tell me about the visions."

"Once I was praying in the Spirit, and I had a vision of a golden vessel."

"Like a ship?"

"Like a vase or a container. It was on a cloth of purple silk. There was an angel there, and he was holding out his hands."

"What did the vision mean?"

"For a long time I didn't know what the vision meant. But then my friend who is a prophetess—quietly, quietly a prophetess, like, literally, hardly anybody knows. She said it was a message about being a vessel for the Spirit, and about a royal calling, but I had to give myself to it."

"That's why you write the magazine articles?"

"That's why I'm writing the books. That's why I'm traveling around so much. To speak into people's hearts and lives."

"But you like it, too. You're good at it. You don't want to work at a desk job."

"That's true. I don't want to be chained to a desk. I was made this way for a reason."

"Any other visions?"

"Yes."

"Tell me."

"Another time. Later."

"All right. It's a lot to risk, right? Telling me all these things?"

"It's nothing to risk. I already have given myself over to all of it."

"I can wait. I want to get to know you."

"Would you hold me now?"

"Yes."

"Don't come over here inside my blanket. You stay inside your blanket and I'll stay inside my blanket, and you can hold me that way, with the separate blankets."

•

"Do you like it here?"

"I'm uncomfortable here."

"Why?"

"I don't like the cold, and I don't like all the soldiers in their uniforms, and I don't like all the military songs. I think I might be a pacifist."

"But these are the men and women who give their lives to keep us free."

"I like watching the football game, and I don't mind cheering for Air Force, but I am uncomfortable with the whole martial atmosphere. It seems to me to have a lot to do with death and killing."

"But sacrificial death and killing, don't you think? Not death or killing that anyone wants to do."

"I don't know if that's true. That's what basic training is for, I think. To break down the part of a person's conscience where they have this inhibition against killing, so they can want to kill, so they can kill at will, to save their lives or save their buddy or fulfill their mission."

"I think that's a selfish way to think about it. Because it's because of these guys and gals here that you have the freedom to say something like that."

"I can't deny it. I know that's true. That complicates the way I feel about it."

"You are shivering. Here, let's combine our blankets."

"Can we put them under our legs, too, because these bleachers are so cold."

"You know, if you moved out here with me, I wonder if you could take the cold all winter, if this is what it does to you."

"Are you really here for good? I mean, you were in Florida, and now you're here, and you've been back and forth. But maybe you would just end up back in Florida."

"I don't want to be anchored anyplace. I want to be free to move around. But I like cold places. I wouldn't mind moving to Alaska. My aunt has a hotel in Alaska. I like the idea of spending some time there with her, helping her run it for a while."

"What if you—even we—had children? Wouldn't you want to stay put for a while, for the sake of stability?"

"I don't want to have children, ever. I mean, I love children. I think I would be an okay mother. But the things I'm meant to do with my life would, I think, make it very difficult to have children."

"I didn't know this about you, that you wouldn't want children. It surprises me."

"This is why it's good, I think, you came out here. We need to sort these things out. We need to find out if we love each other."

"I feel like you're holding some things back."

"That's true, but here we are, and I want to watch this football game since I paid forty bucks each for the tickets."

•

"Is it okay with you if I put my hand on your knee while I drive?"

"Yes. I'm very happy that you put your hand on my knee."

"It's interesting, you know. Whenever I relate to you in a physical way, you respond very positively. But whenever I relate to you in a spiritual way, it gets complicated, and I don't know how to read you, exactly."

"I feel like in some ways they are different issues."

"I don't think they are in any way separable."

"I feel like the physical expressions of love are very important and they mean something."

"I don't disagree. That's why I won't let you kiss me."

"But it's strange. You will let me do other things that seem to me to be more intimate than kissing is."

"I feel like if you and me were kissing, I would be giving myself over to you in a way that I'm not ready to do."

"Why is that?"

"Because I think that spiritually we are in very different places. I think you're open to spiritual things, but I don't think that you are really very far along. And I can't tell if you are open to them because you really desire them or if you are just open to them because you want to be closer to me."

"That's a fair question to raise. I don't know, either, sometimes. There's a lot of things going on very quickly, and it can be confusing to me."

"Also, I don't know if I love you."

"Do you think love is some kind of lightning flash? Like it strikes you and then the reverberations just ring out forever?"

"That's how love is with God, I think. And I think that's one thing you haven't really entered into the fullness of."

"I think that maybe love is a choice that people make."

"That's not very romantic."

"I don't know what good romance is, sometimes. I mean, it's good to be romantic, and it's good to have feelings. But I've had feelings for people before, and they've had feelings for me, but what was lacking, I think, was a choice to make a life together. A commitment."

"It's very scary to me to hear you speak that way. Because it seems very mechanical to me. It seems in keeping with many of the things that seem cold about you, to me. Everything seems so reasoned, so calculated. It makes me think that everything about the way you approach me must be some kind of calculation."

"If that were true, though, wouldn't I just tell you everything you wanted to hear all the time? It seems to me evidence of good faith that we have these kinds of conversations all the time, and that we have these, for lack of a better word, arguments, or disagreements."

"I don't enjoy arguing or disagreeing."

"Me either."

"I'm just going to keep my hand on your leg here, except when I have to shift gears, until we get up to the top of the mountain, okay? I just want to enjoy the ride and enjoy you and enjoy this kind of closeness while we look at the mountains and enjoy the creation and all its wonder. It's not a slight to you. It's just something I need right now, if it's all right with you. But I want to keep my hand on your leg, okay?"

"Of course. I love that you have your hand on my leg. It is really nice."

•

"That right there is called Witch's Titty."

"Why?"

"Because look at it. It looks like a Witch's Titty."

"Yeah. I guess it does."

"You know what I think whenever I pass this place?"

"Tell me."

"There was this dance in high school, and there was this boy, let's call him Bob, he asked me to this dance. He was a senior and I was a freshman. I got all dressed up and he got me a corsage. When you go with a senior and you're a freshman, it's exciting, you know, because he picked you. You're the one he picked, and he passed over older girls to pick you. And before I left, my dad told him he could keep me out until midnight but no later. And he kissed me on the cheek, my dad, and he said I love you and we trust you, me and your mother. So we went to this dance, and it was all right. There was music, there was food, there was dancing. And afterward, I wanted this guy, Bob, to kiss me. It was something I really wanted. I had built it up big time in my mind. He drove me out to this park I'm going to take you to later, out by the ski lifts. It was the place where all the kids went to sit in their cars and make out. We had to drive past Witch's Titty to get there. And I knew that was why we were going to this park, and it was okay with me. But when we got there, this guy, Bob, he started acting really nervous. He was staring straight ahead and he started sweating at his forehead. I felt sorry for him because I could tell he was very nervous. Then he said, like he was apologizing, 'This is just something I really have to do.' And he leaned toward me and I thought he was going to kiss me. But then he put his hands up my dress. I wanted to say no to him but I was so surprised I guess my voice caught in my throat. And then I put my hand down there to push his hand away and he grabbed my wrist and held it so hard it bruised a ring around my wrist where he was holding it. Then he put his hand in my panties and he stuck his finger up inside me and poked around. It didn't hurt. It didn't feel good, either, but it didn't hurt. Then he just held his finger in there like that for a while and moved it around. Then he drove me home."

"What did you do?"

"I didn't do anything. I went inside and went to bed and stared at the ceiling for a long time. It wasn't until a lot later that I cried."

"So nothing happened to him?"

"He's still around. We became friends again later. I forgave him."

"I don't forgive him."

"You don't have to. But that's something you'll have to work on. Unforgiveness. Like the things you sometimes say about your mother."

"I just feel protective of you. I don't like it that for him there were no consequences."

"You carry the consequences around inside yourself, don't you?"

"Me or him?"

"Something about you reminds me of him sometimes."

"That makes me feel terrible that you would say that."

"I just think there's things you should know about me if we are really going to think about being together."

"Is that what we're doing?"

"It's just something I thought of because we were driving by Witch's Titty. That's all."

•

"When a long time passes like this and you're so quiet, I wonder what you're thinking."

"Do you think you have the right to know what I'm thinking?"

"I had a girlfriend in college one time who used to say things like that. She used to say, 'You know what I like about my thoughts? They're mine. I don't have to share them with you.'"

"Did she say that after you were prying at her to give up her thoughts?"

"Usually, yes."

"All right. What do you want to know?"

"So many things."

"You choose one thing. Any one thing. I'll tell you."

"One thing. Okay, the visions. You told me one time you would tell me more about the visions."

"You see this here?"

"What? The road? The mountains? The sky?"

"The motion, through space. Through time, too. Once I was driving this road, and I had a vision of motion through space and through time."

"While you were driving?"

"I saw all of creation as though it were a liquid, and we were swimming through it. Me, and all the creatures, land creatures and water creatures, too. The water was a deep blue, sparkling, but also translucent. You could see through it. And the rock faces were shimmering like precious jewels."

"Was this a distraction while you were driving?"

"It was almost as if I were no longer driving anymore. I had given up control and although in the physical world my hands were on the wheel, and even though in the vision I was moving through a space not unlike the one we are moving through right now, and even though I had given up control, and even though there was that drop-off there just out your window, a couple thousand feet, maybe, I wasn't afraid. What I was mostly was in awe."

"Was it like you imagined seeing these things, or was it like you actually were moving through these things."

"It was physically real. I could even smell the perfume of it."

"What did it smell like?"

"There was a sweetness to it. There was a honey and almond quality to it."

"Was the car moving through it, too?"

"The car went away. It was just my body being carried forward on the current of it."

"Sometimes when you talk about these things, I want to believe you, and I want to understand, because I do believe you, but it is very hard to believe you, and it is very hard to try to know how to understand."

"Because you aren't yet seeing with the eyes of the Spirit."

"Because I haven't had experiences like this, and I've never known anyone else who has. There is a certain light that gets in your eyes when you talk about them, and it is a little bit frightening to me."

"That's something you have to let go of."

"Maybe so, but I don't know how."

"You do it by doing it."

"That's easy to say, but if it were easy to do, wouldn't many other people do it? If nothing else, to speak the tongues of angels and harvest the gold dust and sell it at market rate?"

"When you speak of it that way, it makes me angry."

"I don't mean to make you angry, and I am not making fun. I like you and possibly want to love you. I'm just trying to look at what you're saying from all different directions and turn it over in my mind that way."

"That's not letting go. That's holding onto control."

"I don't know what to say."

"Maybe it would be better not to say anything else for a while."

"Okay. All right. Okay."

•

"Rise and shine."

"I'm so tired."

"It's morning."

"It's dark."

"The idea is to hit the slopes early."

"Really, I'm wiped. I'm sorry."

"I'm turning on the light."

"Please don't. Really. I don't know if it's the altitude or the nonstop going or just maybe general emotional exhaustion. I'm not trying to bail out on you. I'm still willing to ski. But my body doesn't want to get up so early right now, and I feel like I should listen to it so I don't get sick."

"It smells like sickness in here. Your breath has a sinus quality to it."

"That's what I'm talking about."

"The only way out is through. Please, get up. Let's ski."

"You know people there. Why don't you go on without me, and let me catch up with you this afternoon."

"Really?"

"Please understand."

"Really? This is really the choice you are making?"

"Please?"

•

"There are many ways in which I feel more like your mother than like a person with whom you might be falling in love."

"This is because I didn't go skiing this morning."

"It's so many things. You are, I have come to believe, a fundamentally passive person."

"What do you mean?"

"Like it was me who drove all the way here from Colorado Springs."

"I can't drive a stick shift."

"I offered to teach you."

"Don't you think it would be horrible to try to learn while driving up the steepest mountains in the whole country?"

"Those are in Alaska."

"Those drop-offs, though."

"But that's a spirit of fear."

"That's a spirit of safety. I want to be safe. I want you to be safe. I don't mind learning to drive a stick, but I want to learn in a parking lot."

"I have to ask you to clean up after I make dinner, or to do the dishes."

"We're staying in all these houses where friends of yours are out of town for the winter. I don't know what I should and shouldn't be touching or when it is an imposition to take the initiative. It's a situation where I feel like you're in the driver's seat and I'm mostly taking my cues from you."

"I'm thinking about gender roles here. It seems to me like the man should be taking the leadership roles in a relationship. But you are always taking your cues from me. I am the de facto leader, even though I am a woman."

"There have been many instances where I have tried to take the lead, but you have made it clear that you don't like the choice I make."

"That's what I mean by passive. You just concede the high ground to me."

"I don't think you would respond well to being strong-armed."

"With love you have to do it. With love."

"To me the more loving thing would be more of a give and take. More of a partnering kind of thing."

"I feel like because you are so passive that one day the anger is going to come spilling out. I feel like you don't tell me when you are really angry."

"I have only one time been angry, but I knew it wasn't right to be angry, so I didn't say anything about it to you."

"When?"

"When you were still living in Florida and you went to visit that guy in North Carolina and you rode on the back of his motorcycle and you called me and told me what a good time you were having there on the back of his motorcycle."

"That's true. That was fun. Really, truly fun. I loved visiting him, and I loved going for a ride on his motorcycle."

"That made me angry, but I didn't say anything because I didn't feel like I had the right to say anything because I don't own you, we aren't committed, you have the right to make your own choices."

"So why get angry?"

"Because I wanted you to be having fun with me and not that guy on that motorcycle."

"You don't own a motorcycle."

"I don't even like motorcycles. People I knew kept getting killed on motorcycles."

"So you were worried about me getting killed?"

"No, I was mostly worried about you having fun. And one other thing."

"What?"

"I know some women who had orgasms from riding motorcycles. I had a picture of you with your arms around his waist, riding those mountain roads, holding onto him, having an orgasm."

"So you weren't concerned about whether I was going to get killed?"

"Did you have an orgasm?"

"Of all of the questions you should never have asked, this is the number one question you never should have asked."

•

"Your flight leaves in six hours, so I think we ought to leave in three. That gives us an hour to get to the airport and an hour for security and baggage and another hour cushion in case we hit bad traffic."

"Let me finish packing my things and then do you want to have dinner together before I leave?"

"You can have dinner at the airport, and it's too early anyway, don't you think? I don't think I'll be hungry until much later."

"The reason I was thinking dinner was I have a feeling that after today we may not keep seeing each other anymore."

"I haven't decided about that yet."

"If that is what happens, I want to spend one last nice time with you and let you know that I cared about you and that I care about you."

"That's something I want, too. I'm going into the bedroom and lie down while you finish packing. I'm tired, and I know you're tired. When you're done packing, why don't you come into the bedroom and lie down and rest?"

•

"I love holding you."

"Shh."

"I mean it. This is something I will take with me when I leave."

"Shh."

•

"The reason I can't let you kiss me is the same reason as always. Even though right now I want you to kiss me. Do you understand?"

"I don't understand."

"I want you to understand. I don't want you to be hurt."

"I will be hurt, but let's not talk about it right now and interrupt what is nice."

"Will you do one thing for me? When we get to the airport?"

"Yes?"

"When you go through the gate, and you want to turn around and look at me, don't look back."

"I know what it means, for you to say that to me now."

"Shh. Put your face against mine. Touch your face to mine."

"I don't know what to say."

"Don't say anything. Just put your face against my face."

"Language fails."

"Just close your eyes and let go for a while. Let's be together. Let's be."

"But what does it mean?"

"You don't have to understand what it means. I don't understand what it means. It's not less beautiful if you don't understand it."

"I want it to mean when we get to the gate I'm going to turn around and take one last look at you."

"Shh."

"So I can remember you until the next time I see you."

"Shh."

"I love the way it feels, being so close to you."

"No more words."

SEVEN STORIES ABOUT
SEBASTIAN OF
KOULÈV-VILLE

1. The First Day I Met Sebastian

THE CHILDREN AT THE ORPHANAGE SAID Sebastian is a liar.

The man at the tree place said Sebastian is the best translator in Ouest Province. No French in his English.

The missionaries said, Sebastian is bad news. When he was a child he was always breaking things. You should see the two ladies who raised him. They're both hunched over. He wore them out.

The Canadian dentist recommended Sebastian. He said one day he was up in the mountains doing field dentistry, and this husband and wife came in with vampire teeth. Triangles that came to points. They said their teeth hurt, and Sebastian said, "Don't fix the vampire teeth. Just do the fillings." But the dentist didn't listen. He restored the man's teeth and the woman's teeth to happy squares. He showed them in the mirror. He thought they'd be so happy. But the woman yelled and the man cried. Sebastian listened and did his translating. Sebastian said, "Get out the file. They want the vampire teeth back. There's a thing they do." The man pulled the neck of his shirt to his shoulder. There were hundreds of little scars, some of them fresh.

I paid Sebastian seventy dollars a day. The other translators got fifty, but he said he had a thing for sevens. He said he had seven older brothers. When he was seven days old, seven women begged his father not to give him away to the two lady missionaries. They said seven curses will befall him.

"The first curse was the curse of English," Sebastian said. We were walking the village Barette, taking the census of the rabbits and the chickens. "No Creole allowed. No French. Only English."

He spoke in English, read in English, wrote in English, watched movies in English, gave tours of the missionary compound to visiting Americans and Danes in English. "They said, we're your mothers now," he said. "Children speak the language of their mothers."

The day he turned seventeen, the two missionary ladies drove him up the mountain to his father's house. They said, "Now you're grown. We've done all we can." Sebastian said, "Aren't you my mothers?" They cried and drove away. His father came out of the house and cried and embraced him and spoke to him in a language he couldn't understand. "The second curse was the curse of Creole," Sebastian said. "It took me seven years to speak it well enough to pass for a Haitian."

Up the hill was the houngan's house. His wooden roof was painted purple beneath a field of orange stars. I wanted to visit him and convince him to sell it to me to take to Florida. Sebastian said, "If the houngan came to my village, we would have to kill him."

"Why?" I said.

"Because," Sebastian said, "he does not have the love of Christ in his heart."

Later, I asked the elders of Sebastian's village if they would kill the houngan. They laughed. "Sebastian is a liar," they said. "The houngan is our friend. He goes to the church in Barette sometimes on Sundays when they need a trumpet player. The houngan is a good trumpet player."

In the village Barette, Sebastian told me the third, fourth, fifth, sixth curses. It was getting dark, and we were walking up out of the village. I asked him what was the seventh curse. "You see these people, all my neighbors? I have to live among them. You and me, we're not like them."

He headed up the hill a ways, and I followed him across the mountain to his home. From every house we passed, people called their greetings.

2. Before the Earthquake

This was before the earthquake reduced the Hotel Montana to rubble. We were sitting at the bar drinking Dominican beers. Jean-Pierre, Sebastian, and me. The next morning we had to drive to Jacmel to count some rabbits and chickens. Sebastian had a little cocaine, and I gave him a little money, and he gave me the cocaine, and I put it in my pocket for the morning.

We were playing a game called Who's More Heroic Than the Americans. It was a joke of a game. The first round everyone said: "Everyone who's not an American." The second round you had to tell another true story, but this one had to be specific.

"I knew a Catholic priest in Cité Soleil," Jean-Pierre said. "He was Nigerian. The people were so mean to him. This went on for years. They stole things from his house. Once, he was beaten in the street and no one came to his aid. Still, he lived seven years in a shanty house, even though he could have lived well. He could have lived anywhere. One day a little retarded boy was crossing an open sewer on a lashed-together bridge made of two halves of one tree. The sewer was five feet deep with water and every kind of human waste. People pissed in it, shit in it. The sewer was the color of disease. This little retarded boy couldn't have been more than five years old. Halfway across the bridge, some older boys came and shook both sides, just to be mean. The little retarded boy fell in. He was flailing around. There was a big crowd. People were watching him go down, but nobody wanted to jump in. Around the time the boy went over, the Nigerian priest came walking by. He didn't even hesitate. He didn't take off his clothes or his watch or take out his wallet or anything. He just jumped in, head-first, into the shitwater. He went under and came back up with that kid. That brown sludge was in his mouth, in his teeth, in his eyes."

"I can beat that," Sebastian said. "I knew a man who took a blowtorch to the side of a shipping container somebody was using for a store in the village Marigot. The store owner caught him red-handed at midnight. His bag was filled up with biswuit, dry goods, Tampico juices, Coca-Colas. The store owner called for his cousins, and his cousins called for their cousins. Soon all the men of the village surrounded this man in the shipping container. They tied him up, and in the morning they dragged him out into the middle of the road. They brought out all the children to see. The store owner said, 'See what happens when you steal.' While the man was still alive, they hacked off his fingers and toes one by one with a machete. They sealed the wounds with a hot iron. Then they hacked off his feet and hands. Then they hacked off his arms at the elbows and his legs at the knees. Then they poured gasoline over his head and set him on fire and watched him dance around while he died."

"The store owner was a hero," Jean-Pierre said, "for protecting his family business."

"No," Sebastian said. "The thief was a hero, for risking his life to get food for his family."

They looked at me. I shielded my part of the table with my arm. I poured some of the powder on the table, made a line, and snorted. I said, "I wish I had some to share."

3. After the Earthquake

We went down to the mausoleum where Sebastian's dead were buried. The earth had buckled in waves, and one of the waves split the center of the concrete, and where it had split, the fresh corpses had fallen out of their graves and mingled on the ground with the bones of the longer dead, and some carrion animals were pulling at a dead woman's face. The smell is in my nostrils still.

At the graveside, I told Sebastian I couldn't take this gruesome scene, this horror movie.

Sebastian lifted the bodies from the ground one by one, and held them for a while. "Auntie Marie," he said. "Auntie Ti-ti. Auntie Solange."

4. The Pig and the Pony

We reached a vista. All of Port-au-Prince stretched out beyond us, the sun reflecting from the metal roofs of the bidonville shanties like a hundred thousand daytime stars. An American Airlines jet took off from the airport. Sebastian said any child with a shoulder-fired rocket launcher could stand on any rooftop in La Saline and blow any airplane out of the sky. Why hadn't it happened yet?

A donkey draped with yellow saddlebags came up the road from the distance. A thin man in a yellow shirt led the donkey up the hill. He waved as he got closer. His shirt and the saddlebags said DHL in red letters. We said *bonswa* and *komon ou ye* and *byen, byen*. "What do you have?" Sebastian said. "Letters," the DHL courier said. "Where is your motorcycle?" Sebastian said. The DHL courier said the gas tank had rusted out, so he had replaced it with a gallon milk jug, but someone had dropped a match into the milk jug while he was making a delivery at the cement store.

After the DHL courier left, six men came up the hill carrying a casket. They were dressed in fine linen suits, and white specks from the dirt in the road were soiling their shoes, which were newly shined. We made room so they could pass us, and as they passed we briefly joined in their funeral song.

We watched them disappear behind a bend where the road followed the curve of the mountain, and when they were gone, I asked Sebastian who was in the casket. "That is the wife of one of the elders of the village Jean-Baptiste," he said. "She fell in love with a bourgeois man in the city. Every day she took the tap-tap to see him. He gave her so much money. When the elder found out, he fed her feet to his pony."

Later I visited the village Jean-Baptiste and played soccer with some of the men who lived there. After the game, the women made a feast of rice and stewed tomatoes and a sauce of leeks and carrots. For me, they killed their fattest rabbit, and they would not take any money for it. While we were eating, I asked about the elder who fed his wife's feet to a pony. A man stood up and said, "Come, let me show you." We walked down the orange path, past his sister's house, his brother's house, the houses of his two friends and his one sworn enemy. A bone-thin pony was tied up in the front of his own house. He petted the pony, and said, "The lies they are telling about you." Then we went to the back yard, where he kept two pigs, and he pointed to the fatter one. "It was this fellow who ate the feet," he said. "Not the pony."

We stared at the pig for a long time. I imagined the woman's feet in its mouth. Then the man laughed bitterly. "Do you think this is a village where we feed the parts of people to animals?" He said it to shame me.

When I told Sebastian, he said, "Don't believe it. I don't trust that pony."

5. The Third, Fourth, Fifth, and Sixth Curses

Once, late at night, we were trying to sleep in the reclined seats of a borrowed Jeep in the middle of the treeless forest, on our way to cross the Dominican border. We both kept machetes under the seats, and I had a gun. Somewhere near enough to hear but not near enough to see, a lot of people were singing and beating drums. I kept the keys in the ignition.

Sometime before morning, Sebastian said, "Tell me about your mother."

"She was a good woman," I said, "but for twenty years she refused to talk to her sister."

"Her sister slept with her husband?" Sebastian said.

"No," I said. "It was a misunderstanding. Her sister forgot to pick me up from school one afternoon, and one time she left me alone in her house for a half hour while she went to the store to buy some groceries. There was an incident with somebody saying something to somebody else about what somebody else said to some other person. I'm not sure I understand it."

"After I was born, my mother ran away," Sebastian said. "No one knows where. There was some kind of craziness in her family. My father said many of them had been turned into zombies. He took me to see them near Furcy. They were chained to a plow, four of them, and pulling it. My father said, 'That's vodou,' and I said, 'No, it's not. That's mental illness.' The farmer had a whip, but he wasn't driving them with it. He didn't need the whip. Their spirits were broken already. They were machines with broken brains."

He reached under his seat for his water bottle and took a sip. "Why are people so bad to each other?" he said. "There was this crazy woman. She always came into town with this mongrel dog. She only had one friend. He was a crazy person, too. A line of drool always hung from his mouth. He had gums instead of teeth.

Sometimes he stole some food for her dog. I never saw her eat. She was always looking for food for the dog."

Sometimes when I think of him, now, it's this moment. He's staring out the window in the direction of the mountains of Massif de la Selle, thinking about his mother.

"Sometimes she slept on the steps of the mission school. When she did, we stepped over her. Someone might poke her with his foot, to wake her. Someone probably kicked her sometime, but I never saw anyone do it.

"One morning the dog was gone. She was walking the street, looking for the dog. All day she was looking. The next morning, she lay on the steps of the mission school. I stepped over her. We all stepped over her. Nobody poked or kicked her. We let her sleep. We felt sorry for her, because of the dog.

"She was still lying there at the end of the school day, when they opened the doors and let us free. She didn't move the whole day, and then she didn't move the whole night. One of the teachers came along and covered her body with a black sheet. Nobody wanted to take her body. Nobody wanted her to live forever with their own dead. Nobody wanted her bones with their bones.

"Nobody claimed her body until the next morning. It was the crazy man who fed her dog. He lifted her body, sheet and all. He was talking to her. He had her under the armpits, and he started spinning with her. He was dancing with her. They were turning and turning. He was making a noise like an animal soon to the slaughter.

"People were yelling. Put her down, put her down! The boys picked up rocks and threw rocks at him. He had to flee. He tried to carry her away with him, but she was too heavy. The rocks were still coming. His face was bloody from them, and his shirt was torn. Finally, he dropped her in the grass by the side of the road. She lay there for three days, and then a Dutch man paid to have her buried in another village. He sent two men to collect her body.

"For a while I didn't think about her much. But after I saw her relatives chained to the plow, I thought: Could that crazy woman have been my mother?"

6. The Tumor

The kids at the orphanage said, why do you ride around with Sebastian?

The missionaries said, watch out. He wants things from you. He will steal things from you. Watch your guns. Watch your jewelry.

The man at the tree place told me about a cash-for-charcoal scam that ended in nobody getting any charcoal. The man at the art kiosk across the street from the mission told me about a middleman scheme. The man who built the wooden A-frame houses that were meant as temporary housing, but which the people who bought or received them meant to last a hundred years, told me about a strike-and-extortion scheme, which yielded nothing. "I have a hundred bodyguards," the man said, although he only had two. A farmer in Artiste told me of a scam where Sebastian tried to sell electricity he was stealing by tying barbed wire to the new power lines the president was running up the mountainsides. "Does he think I don't have barbed wire?" the farmer said. "Everyone has barbed wire."

Almost every day, Sebastian asked me for more money. He said his nephew needed money to give the school for photocopies. He said his niece needed money for needle and thread. He said the church needed money for sound equipment. He said his father needed money for a saw and a lathe and a level, so he could start a new business as a carpenter. He said he knew a man whose father had a tumor the size of a small grapefruit on his prostate. He said he needed money to take out the tumor and the prostate. "Let me see this man," I said. "Take me to see this man."

We walked down into Sebastian's village. "Don't be alarmed,"
Sebastian said, "when you see their eyes." All the members of the
family had a degenerative eye disease. They all went blind by age
twenty-five. "My friend is twenty-three," Sebastian said. "You can
see it already. The disease is eating his eyes."

There were eight small children, two teenage girls, Sebastian's
friend, and his father and mother, both of whom were in their sev-
enties. Sebastian's friend was a very late child. ("A miracle child," I
said. "A shame and a burden," Sebastian said.) The teenage girls and
the children were the sons and daughters of sons and daughters
and grandsons and granddaughters who had long since fled for the
city. These were the unwanted children, or the too-many children,
or the children taken early by the blindness. Sebastian's friend was
working for tips at the Hotel Kinam to bring in money, and tending
the garden in the mornings. When he was gone, people stole from
the garden. There was no one in the family able enough to do anything about it.

We greeted Sebastian's friend. "My friend," he said, "my good
friend. You will come see my father."

He led us through a maze of banana trees, past the hundred-
year-old stone house, to the unfinished concrete house at the back
of the property. It had holes for windows and a hole where the roof
would go. The old man sat shaking in a chair at the center of the one
room. Piles of construction sand filled the four corners.

The old man leaned on his cane and shook. He waved us near
him and spoke. He had the breath of brown death. After he said half
a sentence, he paused to catch his breath, and Sebastian translated.
"I saw you in a dream," he said. "Bondye sent you from America.
Your journey took you over the sea. You are estranged from your
mother. You are wearing glasses and you have beautiful shoes."
Most of these things were true. "Bondye said this man will come,"
he said. "You will show him your wound. He will lay hands on your
wound, and your wound will be healed."

He pushed on his cane. With some effort, he sat upright in his chair. With his shaking hand, he handed the cane to his son. With great effort, he reached both hands to his pants button and his zipper. He said, "I will show you." He unbuttoned his pants, and he unfastened his zipper. With both hands, as if presenting a bouquet of flowers, he held himself out to us. What he showed was mostly tumor. His penis and his testicles had shriveled to a flaccid tininess. Most of his hair had fallen away. Only a slight smear of peach fuzz remained, and it was slick with a yellowish-white discharge from a suppurating wound that was on the tumor but not of the tumor.

"Bondye said," the old man said again, "this man will come. You will show him your wound. He will lay hands on your wound, and your wound will be healed."

Everyone was looking at me. Sebastian, with his good eyes. The man's son, with his cataracting, failing eyes. The old man, with his blind eyes. Even the tumor seemed like a giant dying eye. The man's son was nodding, as if to say: Go ahead. Sebastian was watching, as if to see what kind of man I was after all our time together.

I held out my hands. I cupped them as if I were preparing to draw water from the river. I put them on either side of the tumor. My right wrist grazed the old man's tiny penis, and my left wrist grazed his testicles. The skin swollen by the tumor was hot, and the skin covering the genitals was as cold as a slab at the morgue. "You must pray," the son said. "Our Father, who art in heaven," I said. It wasn't a prayer to the sky. It was a prayer to the people in the room. If there was any belief to borrow, it was all theirs.

Then I couldn't remember the rest of the words to the prayer, even though it was the most famous prayer in the world. In my mind, it had become conflated with a less famous poem, by an American who had once been my teacher at the university. *Our Father who art in heaven, I am drunk. Again. Red wine. For which I offer thanks. I ought to start with praise, but praise comes hard to me. I stutter . . .*

I had not memorized the whole poem, but I did remember the ending, the beautiful ending. The drunk, praying, thinks of himself as an old-time cartoon character, a poor jerk who wanders out on air and then looks down. Below his feet, he sees eternity, and suddenly his shoes no longer work on nothingness, and down he goes. The drunk prays: *As I fall past, remember me.*

It seemed as fitting a prayer as the one I had forgotten. I cobbled together bits and pieces of both, and drew on the language of special pleading I remembered from all those dreary years at the Cherry Road Baptist Church. I used the words suppurating, and grapefruit, and hot and cold, and shrivel and shrink.

When I was done, nothing happened. Everyone was as blind or cataracted or tumored or lying or despicable as we had been before we prayed, and my hands were wet with white and yellow pus. I told the old man I was sorry. Nothing happened. He had not been healed. I must not be the man Bondye had sent from over the sea. He said, "We must wait. Bondye's time is not our time."

Outside, I asked Sebastian, "How much is the surgery."

Sebastian said, "All surgeries are three hundred dollars."

I said, "I have four hundred dollars in my pocket. I'm going to give all of it to him."

Sebastian said, "If you give him four hundred dollars for his surgery, they will use it to buy sand and Portland. Or they will use it to buy a window. Or they will use it to buy corrugated aluminum for a roof. The old man will die soon no matter what you do."

"What can I do?" I said.

"You can give the money to me," Sebastian said. "I will take it to pay the doctor, and I will pay the tap-tap to take him to the doctor."

I looked at him, and I knew. He would take the money and put it in his pocket, and I would never see him again. Or I would see him again the next time he wanted some money.

"No," I said, quietly. "No, no."

I put the money back in my pocket and vowed to return after we did the count in Mirebalais—in three weeks. Pick up the old man myself. Take him to the hospital myself. Pay for the surgery myself.

In later years, a woman told me: Who do you think you are, to play God? Who do you think you are, the savior of the world? I said: I only wanted to save this one man for a little while. I knew he was going to die soon.

Three weeks passed. We returned to the village. Another casket, a cheap one, was marching up the street. So many of the pallbearers were blind. "Don't worry," Sebastian said. "You took his tumor in your hands." "But I didn't cut it out," I said. "You should have given me the money," he said.

7. At the Marché

A few days later we went to the Marché en Fer to buy fruits and vegetables. The whole market had fallen down in the earthquake, but now an Irishman had rebuilt the clock tower and the minarets, restored the masonry, and reinforced the iron columns. The Irishman said the new walls were earthquake-proof, and the roof was covered with solar panels.

These were the days when it was hard to walk into a building and not be afraid the walls and the roof might fall on you and crush your head. You looked for a space beside a sturdy piece of furniture, and traced an invisible line at a forty-five degree angle, which you'd dive beneath for shelter at the first shake. Every so often, continuing to this day, another building would fall in an aftershock. All over the country we saw three-story buildings pancaked to one story, and lo these years later, the bodies still inside. They didn't even stink anymore. Almost for certain, the bacteria and the worms and the rodents had picked them to bones.

But it wasn't like the early days. People were moving. Children in uniforms walked to school in the mornings. The tap-taps were full of men carrying their work tools in canvas bags. In the city, the cell phone vendors walked the streets in their red smocks and carrying their red phones, selling rechoj cards, and soda and water vendors walked through the traffic jams, carrying on their heads cardboard boxes full of plastic sugar-and-caffeine concoctions and vacuum-sealed plastic bags of water.

In the Marché, I bought two bottles of Atomic Energy Drink, one for me and one for Sebastian, and he bought me a styrofoam container full of griot and fried plantains and pikliz. I bought him a pizza from a vendor billing herself as the Walt Disney Pizza Company. Famous mice and dogs and ducks decorated the sign behind her.

We took our food outside and crouched in the shade of the nearest wall. While we were eating, Sebastian said, "When you leave, will you come back?"

I stopped eating for a moment. An uncharacteristic sincerity was in his eyes. I didn't trust it.

"You are my good friend," he said.

But that's what everyone said. Everyone who wanted something. I could see myself, in a few weeks, sitting on my couch in Florida, watching football. The job was over. There was no reason for me to stay. "What will you do," I said, "after I leave."

He patted his wallet, where he kept some of his walking-around money, and he patted his shoe, where he kept the rest. "I have met some important people," he said. He pointed at every ten degrees of the sky around us. "I'm going to buy a new suit. The future is big."

Already he had gathered ten of the best English speakers in Koulèv-Ville. He planned to drill them six days a week, in the mornings, when the mind is still fresh. He planned to lease them by the day, to journalists and tourists and aid organizations of every stripe, with special rates for weekly or monthly hires. He would take twenty percent, as his fee. No longer would he be the wage worker. Now he would be the collector of the real money, the wage-giver, the big boss.

"When you get home," Sebastian said, "you will not remember me."

Within six months, he would be dead. The rally at the Palace. The fires. The burning tires. The gunshots, two to the head.

That day at the Marché, he said, "It's going to be the most beautiful suit. It's going to be linen. It's going to be chalk-striped, double-breasted. It's going to have a notched lapel. I'm going to get it tailored."

Q & A

Q: Do you think you can resurrect the dead?

A: I am the fiery angel. I can run time backward. I can speed it up and dance babies back into the womb.

Q: Do our thoughts betray us?

A: Scientists are perfecting a brain scanner that can already show distorted images of your dreams. Then they'll just stick you in an MRI machine and ask the questions you don't want to answer, and your thoughts will betray you. Until then, other people can only guess.

Q: On the cover of this book, it says "Fiction."

A: That's what people write when they want to get away with telling the truth. When they want to convince you of a lie, they dress up some facts and call it "Nonfiction." Either way, people from the past send angry emails.

Q: Did the things in this book actually happen in the unvirtual world, what the kids call meat space?

A: It's like Kazuo Ishiguro said: "I'm more interested in what people tell themselves happened rather than what actually happened."

Q: Don't hide behind Kazuo Ishiguro.

A: I remember the bully who beat me up almost every day in junior high school. I remember the sweet odor of those red mesh equipment bags that held body armor and hung from meat hooks. I remember the puke-green walls of the locker room. I remember the special orange-brown of the rust on the edges of the lockers. I remember the shape of my own hairless testicles, how they seemed to retreat in fear when it was time to take a shower among a bunch of kids my own age or a little older who looked like full-grown men and had a foot or more of height on me. But were they as big as I remember, or was my idea of their height exaggerated because of my smallness and the smallness of my idea of myself and the bigness of my idea of them? And did they beat me up almost every day, or did they just beat me up a few times, but I responded so strongly and fearfully that in my memory it became almost every day? Why am I calling the football pads "body armor"? Had I ever seen a meat hook? Did I think of those red mesh bags as hanging from meat hooks back then, or is that something that I used later, to gild the story—or, no, to uglify the story. Because they're conveniently dramatic words, aren't they? Meat, and hook? They open up associations. The body as meat, the cheapness of meat, the animality of meat. The hook, which pierces and controls.

Q: Who sends the angry emails?

A: People from the Christian school. People from the churches where I was raised and where I worked as a pastor. They follow a form. The first thing the email writer does is to assure me that he or she is reaching out in love to offer correction. Correction is the price of love.

Q: Do you think that's true?

A: If it is, then these awful stories I'm writing are also an expression of love.

Q: How?

A: Because I see them as a correction of the untruths I was told as a child about how the world works.

Q: Are you saying that the adults in your life were liars?

A: No. I think they were mostly good and decent people. I just think that it is inconvenient and possibly destructive, for some people, to closely examine your own life, or to have a reckoning with your past, your family history, your community of origin, your own choices.

Q: Unintentional liars, then?

A: I knew a woman, my teacher. A mentor in many ways. She said the most useful thing: Our job is to identify the distance between the story we've been telling ourselves about our lives— the received story, or the romantic story, or the wishful thinking— and replace it with the story that experience is revealing about our lives, the story that is more true.

Q: The facts are the same in both versions of the story.

A: It's the reckoning that changes. The narrative itself is the reckoning. The choices you make about what is or isn't significant, and what it all comes to mean.

Q: Why do you often tell the same story two or three different ways?

A: It's not done with me yet. I forgot something important, or I hadn't learned it yet.

Q: You still believe in something as old-fashioned as meaning-making?

A: Maybe the biggest fiction I want to create is that it all matters. It matters so much. It matters and matters.

Q: Contrary to the evidence.

A: This is the only life I have. This is the only life you have unless you're lucky enough to die and be resurrected as the fiery angel.

Q: Why do you have the robot in the story about the suicide?

A: It was a mistake. That story needed seventy-three robots, twelve pirates, three Vikings, three zombies, seven murders in polygamist cults, two slow trains to Bangkok, three bejeweled elephants in the court of Catherine the Great, six scarlet-threaded elevators to space, fourteen backlit liquor bars in Amsterdam, five bearded men spinning plates on top of thirty-foot poles in Central Park, four mechanical rabbits, three alarm clocks, two magic tricks, twenty-four test tubes, the Brooklyn Bridge, the London Bridge, the boob doctor's daughter. . . .

Q: Whatever it takes to get your attention?

A: Whatever it takes to cover all the hurt.

Q: Are there any stories you want to try again?

A: Turn the page and see.

THE SWEET LIFE

THE BOY IN THE CASKET was my wife's nephew.

"I want to talk about biscuits," the preacher said.

We were all of us sweating. The sanctuary doubled as a gymnasium.

The preacher took the store-bought biscuits from their wrapping. He put a piece in his mouth and ate. "Mmm, mmm," he said. "Biscuits is one of the sweetest things in the world."

The boy's mother and father sat apart. Soon they would no longer be married.

"Life can be sweet," the preacher said. "Like these buttermilk biscuits. Yes, sir." He took another bite. He wiped his forehead with a white handkerchief.

My wife was holding my hand. My wife's hand was shaking.

"The sweet life," the preacher said. "Is made of bitter parts."

Like the biscuits, he was saying. He seemed as far away as the planet Jupiter. Everything in the sanctuary gymnasium seemed out of proportion. The basketball hoops were flying saucers.

"Two cups all purpose flour," he said. He poured from a paper bag into a Tupperware cup. He licked his finger and put it to the flour and took it to his lips and tongue. He made a sour face. "It's bitter, flour," he said.

A single drop of sweat rolled down my wife's arm and landed on my hand. It felt wet on my hand. I could see the veins. They seemed so large, bulging there like an old person's veins, like my grandmother's. I had a vision of her, in her red housedress, sweating in her trailer, even though she could well afford to run the air conditioner.

"Baking powder," the preacher said. "One tablespoon." He ate and made his cartoon face.

Some people were laughing. Laughing!

"Three quarters of a teaspoon of salt."

My wife was not crying. Maybe her mouth, like mine, was dry. If you suck on the insides of your dry cheeks you can hold the crying in.

"Baking soda. Vegetable shortening. One cup buttermilk." He tasted the buttermilk. Some things, he said, are sweet, even in the time of bitterness.

Amen, somebody was saying. Were they saying Amen? Was it someone, the mother or the father, who had the right to say Amen? Or was it someone else, anyone else in the room—someone who did not have the right to say Amen.

The preacher poured the buttermilk into a glass bowl, and mixed it with the flour, the baking powder and the baking soda and salt and all.

I looked around to see who was saying Amen.

There was a small oven on the stage. A theater prop, not a working oven. The preacher poured the biscuit batter into a silver biscuit tray and pretended to set it baking. Then he moved from sermon to eulogy.

Somehow the smell of biscuits filled the sanctuary gymnasium.

"No one knows why these things happen, but everything happens for a reason. All things work together for good, to them that love God, to them who are called according to His righteousness."

On the front row, the mother sat beside her mother. They were weeping. Perhaps they were finding comfort in the preacher's words. Perhaps everyone but me and my wife were finding comfort in the preacher's words.

"And God, in His good time. . . ."

The boy was dead in the box.

On the stage, the oven timer dinged. A helper delivered a foil wrapped basket of biscuits. The biscuits were warm, brown. Done. The preacher bit into one. His testimony was that the buttermilk was baked well into the biscuit. "A message of hope I have for you," he said. The biscuit was sweet.

The mother was crying. The father sat with his head in his hands. There were grandparents, cousins. A sister. We all of us must have wanted for hope.

The preacher promised a call to salvation. The musicians took their places on stage to play the music that would make more powerful his talk.

In the moment before the musicians started their music, there was a silence. To me the silence seemed our natural state, bitter and forever. There was a burning smell from the oven. I did not want to give it meaning, but we have been conditioned to give everything meaning. Then we began to sing.

II.

"As I Fall Past, Remember Me"

THERE IS NOTHING BUT
SADNESS IN NASHVILLE

I.

ANOTHER SUICIDE. Area Code 615, the caller ID says. I answer and hear my brother's voice. He just found out, and the funeral's tonight. It's the girl with the red streaks in her hair, the seventeen-year-old he brought home to Florida last Thanksgiving who smoked pot on the back porch and blew my brother in the bedroom while my parents prayed over the turkey and waited for them to wake up from their naps. Unlike the last few girls, this one was shy and lovely. She could hardly make eye contact with any adult in the house. When tickled, she doubled over and got teary-eyed. She watched football without complaining. She said she would never be any good at school. I wanted to take her home and adopt her and raise her through college.

It's 380 miles from my brick apartment in Columbus, Ohio, to the funeral home outside Nashville, Tennessee. Six hours or so. "I'll be there in five," I tell my brother. "Stay," he says. I'm already in the car driving. We spend the six hours talking on cell phones. It's a mistake to keep *Johnny Cash at Folsom Prison* playing softly on the in-dash, but it's not less than fitting. "I didn't love her," he says. "I

didn't want to take care of her." He told her so, and she went to the
bowling alley with some lowlifes from the community college. They
passed around X, and she took too much probably on purpose and
it stopped her heart. The word coming down was they were close to
the hospital but didn't take her to the emergency room because they
were afraid of getting arrested. So they let her die. "You know what
her mother told me?" he said. "She said, 'My daughter loved you.
Swear to god you were the only man ever treated her good. Nobody
ever treated me so good in my whole life is what she said. Nobody
will ever treat me so good again.'

"How do you face that?" he said. "How do you walk into that
funeral parlor and let people talk to you like that when what they
ought to do is punch you in the face?" America flies by while he says
these things. Those rusty bridges over the Ohio, and the rows and
rows of tractor-trailers idling in the vast lots in Louisville, and all
the waystations that conjure brief meetings past: the hitchhiker
in Shepherdsville, the stripper in Elizabethtown, the gas station
preacher in Cave City. We meet at a strip mall off Nashville Pike,
where I leave my car, and we ride together in his pickup truck to the
funeral home near her trailer park in Gallatin. The cab has gone
feral. The floorboards are littered with fast-food bags and empty
plastic bottles and torn candy-bar wrappers. His skin is translucent and he is too skinny. "I told the doctor I'm not taking those pills
anymore," he says. "My sleep was all screwed up and I was hearing
voices. It scared the hell out of me." We're flying over potholes and
all the side roads now are dirt.

I wonder if he ended it with her the same reason he pitched
the pills. It's dark now. Somehow we make a wrong turn, then
another and another. Dirt road shortcuts and switchbacks don't
yield much. We stop at a rural jiffy and a Mexican man points us
half a mile down the road. By time we arrive the service is over. We
first take the mother for catatonic in the foyer, but then she raises
up and runs screaming through the sanctuary doors, and toward

the open casket and throws herself over the body. Four of the men, one an ex-husband, pick her up and carry her to a grieving pew. We watch this through the floor-to-ceiling window separating foyer from sanctuary. "Don't go in there," my brother says to me. "I have to do this myself." I watch him through the window.

The frame the window makes puts me in mind of a TV, and me deaf. If there were closed captions, they'd be sending pleasant words. Her family wants to comfort my brother. Their arms around him are fatherly and motherly. Even her mother calms herself and rises to kiss his cheek. When we leave he says, "I am a horrible person." He is not, but there is no use saying. We retire to his house in Murfreesboro and recline in beanbag chairs and stare at the chalkboard walls of his recording studio and don't speak or sleep. A pattern randomizer bounces lines and shapes across a spectrum of bright colors on the monitor beside the TV, which broadcasts chef shows all night from Chicago, Atlanta, and Tokyo. In the morning we eat biscuits and sausage gravy and bacon and cornbread at the Cracker Barrel by the interstate, and try not to talk about her at all. Before I leave town, he says, "It would have been better if it was me instead of her," and what haunts me all the way home is I'm glad it was her instead of him.

2.

Another theft. Another embezzlement. A trail of broken promises from L.A. to Nashville. No reason to say whose story it is or who is telling the story or who went bankrupt or who got evicted, because every visit to Nashville you hear the same stories about different people. At the Sexy Sadie I say this to my brother, and he says, "Liam, tell him a story he hasn't heard before." Liam takes me down to the basement and kicks the wall and some of the mortar falls away. "Only thing holding this place together is the horsehair in the mortar," he says. "This foundation was laid in the Civil War. This basement was a stop on the Underground Railroad. There's still secret tunnels if you knock out that cinderblock right there.

"That's your portal to a whole tiny city. It's a merchant city, and what it's moving is crack, meth, and heroin. Have you ever done coke and stayed up for seventy-two hours straight? Once this black guy pulled up in a limo and took us to this club where everybody was wearing a suit and a tie. He said once you go in there you can't tell anybody what you see and you can't come out for forty-eight hours. I can't tell you what went on inside but I can say there were city councilmen in there, high-ranking police officers, firemen, A&R guys, ministers, hotel guys—and I mean real high-up execs—and prostitutes galore. Nobody could say whore in there. There were these big black bouncers who kept saying respect, respect. Nobody wanted to mess with these guys, and nobody would. I slept for like two days when I got out of there."

He kept on this way throughout the tour of the house. Every room kept secrets, only some of which he knew. In this room, somebody blew somebody. In this room, somebody OD'd. This is the room where that girl took off her clothes and painted her body red. This is the room with the stolen lava lamp. This is the room with the toy piano. Skip the studio, you've spent enough time in there. That's the boringest place. That's my whole life, boring. On and on, and all the way he was promising the highlight of the tour would be the third-floor balcony. Nobody had so much as touched the third-floor balcony in the three years he had run the Sexy Sadie. As a matter of pride, no one would. Three cats had lived up there, and now three cat skeletons. Three cat skulls. But we never made it to the third-floor balcony.

A photographer arrived from Indianapolis. The other two members of the side project arrived carrying borrowed Diesel jeans and tight black Western dress shirts and Liam and my brother and the other two side-project guys changed into them for the photo shoot.

The six of us piled into a black SUV. Liam said he was hungry. We detoured to a soul food place around the corner. Liam said we all had to eat chitlins and we did. We ate and Liam talked and ate. He said his parents were missionaries. He said he was a missionary kid. He ate chitlins and said he fucked eight girls this week. He said somebody blew him while he was doing blow. He said everybody went to sleep and he mixed down two songs overnight so he could free up the console for his own shit. He said don't let anybody fool you, all anybody cares about is their own shit. He left the table for a few minutes and talked to some church ladies drinking coffee two tables over. They gave him hugs before he left their table. He came back and said, "Tell you what. These yellow tablecloths are the shizz."

We got back in the SUV and went around looking for places to take pictures. The photographer said he wanted gritty. Liam said if gritty meant industrial, he could offer a whole city. We stopped first anyway at a practice studio and took some pictures in the practice space where my brother's old band used to rehearse, and he said here's where we kept the piss jar and here's where the guitarist slept while we worked out the drum and bass problems. Liam picked at the acoustic foam on the wall. He said it was expensive but that didn't keep it from being cheap. He said he could get an industrial spray foam that would do a better job for practically nothing, but no one would respect it because what people really care about is that a studio look like some picture of a studio they saw in a poster from a guitar magazine when they were thirteen years old. We went out through the emergency exit, which was propped open. We stepped out into an overgrown field of green grass and green weeds. There was an eight-foot fence behind us and what looked from a distance like a baby's head pushed between the links. "That's it, right there," the photographer said. "That baby doll head. That's it." When we got closer we saw there were baby doll parts all around. Arms and legs and plenty of them, but no other heads. Behind the fence a boarded-up building rose to four stories.

The metal siding that hadn't been stripped away was black with long streaks of brown where the rust was making a meal of it. The side-project guys stood in front of the fence, with Liam in front, and the baby doll head just off-center, and when they were done, the photographer showed them the previews on his digital camera.

Soon they bought a van and went on a club tour and abandoned my brother in a youth hostel in Boston, above a barroom where people were watching World Cup soccer, and fighting, and the band wasn't allowed to play even though they had driven 350 miles to play at the club's invitation. Everybody thought Liam owned the Sexy Sadie, but it burned down, and after it burned down it turned out somebody else owned it. Liam got a co-write on a hit country record and made a lot of money and moved into the building next door to where the Sexy Sadie had burned down and he called the new place the Sexy Sadie. My brother had written the hook for the song but nobody remembered. He said it was because everybody else was high when he wrote the hook. I want my brother to fight for a co-write, but he says life is too short and moves to Chicago for a while.

3.

Another phone call home. Another problem with money. Another problem with women. In Sacramento, somebody offers my brother sixty grand a year to play guitar and sing at Sunday church services and he says no because he doesn't believe in God anymore. He gets a gig with a lady country singer but she fires him because he doesn't play the Steve Miller Band cover the way she likes. For a while he's Britpop and briefly big in Italy and Holland, but this girl who wears denim skirts wants him to quit and marry her and make babies, so he quits, but she asks him to do things he doesn't want to do like choke her while they're having sex, and eventually she leaves him.

The real money's in Christian rock, a scene that's a hammer-blow, every flirtation leaving him for weeks on the beanbag chairs in Murfreesboro after he's been stiffed paychecks, accused of creepiness with underage fans, ratted out to image-conscious A&R guys. He does the same stuff everybody else does. One night he's smoking pot with a teen pop idol while members of her entourage tryst on dingy apartment couches, the next night she's on the late night shows talking about her virginity pledge. What sets my brother apart is he says the same things no matter who is in the room, and most people prefer what passes for the truth to what's actually true. So he calls and says, "Enough. I quit. Enough." No more touring, no more producing, no more engineering, no more songwriting, no more so much as sitting at the bar at Boscos with anybody wearing Diesel jeans, anybody with spiky hair, anybody with eye makeup, anybody in Nashville who's ever been to San Francisco.

He applies for thirtysome jobs and nobody calls for an interview. There's an ad in the classified section of *The Tennessean* for an administrative assistant position at a trucking company an hour out of town, and they don't call either, but he has a feeling, so he gets in his truck and hand-delivers another resume, and then the fiftysomething manager, an ex-cop named Dickie, calls to say why should he hire a musician? Everybody knows musicians aren't dependable, and anyway they leave without giving notice as soon as they get another music gig. My brother says he's not a musician anymore. He was, but not anymore. He says, I'll do anything, I'll sweep your floors, I'll make you coffee, I'll pick your nose.

It's this last thing, this I'll pick your nose, that does it. Who talks like that? Dickie asks. Anybody so unpolished is somebody I can trust. You're not trying to pull the wool over anybody's eyes. I like you. You're a straight shooter. So soon it's eight-hour days, ten-hour days, twelve-hour days, fourteen-hour days. Truckers never rest. The road, the road, the road. My brother does dispatch, payroll, troubleshoots, schedules, oversees the truckers, oversees the warehouse guys, makes sure nobody's falsifying paperwork, makes sure nobody's hitting anybody else over the head with a wrench.

The truckers are contract workers, mostly. They get paid by the mile. They want work and lots of it. Buddy, can you get me a trip? Buddy, can you get me a run? They curse and he curses back. They want to take a load off in the chair by his desk and tell a story, he listens. Buddy, she hit me with a restraining order again. Buddy, she said don't call no more. Buddy, I followed her over to this house and won't you know it's a swingers party. Buddy, you ain't seen a fellow try harder to stay married. Buddy, you ain't seen a fellow cry more. Buddy, I told her you get it out of your system, then you come home to me where you belong. Buddy, you wouldn't believe this little schoolteacher—blonde hair, glasses, teeny tiny mouth—could have some sex fiend hiding inside that little body. Buddy, I'm gonna be a little late, gotta take a run with this honey I met over here by the elementary school. Buddy, I been going down to one of these swinger parties. Private club. Twenty bucks at the door, two-drink minimum. I figure good for the goose is good for the gander. You ever want to come with me, I'll take you down there, you don't have to do nothing, everybody's cool down there, you can keep your shirt and pants on. I don't hardly ever take my shirt and pants off. No, buddy, all I ever do down there is watch. Sometimes I get so sad watching, I'm thinking about her, buddy, parading around some lowlife place like where I'm at, I'm crying in my beer. Last week I was sitting on the couch with this old boy, naked as a jaybird, I'm telling him about my wife, and he says, Friend, I feel real bad for you. Tell you what I'm going to do. I'm going to have my wife here suck your dick. No, buddy, he didn't get off on it or nothing. Decent guy. He just sat there and drank his beer while she done it. Buddy, it felt real good but it didn't keep me from getting lonely. Buddy, I miss her so much. Buddy, I'm gonna go over there right now and see how she's doing. On and on, this talk, and my brother starts to care, and my brother starts going down to the dive bar some nights with the old truckers while they sing karaoke to the old ladies they go home with, and he listens to their stories about wife number four, the one with the kid you start to love so much it's like the kid's your own, and then three wives later, the kid's still like he's your own, and you're sending checks for community college, and you're giving advice, you're giving up the spare bedroom, you're driving cross country to bail him out of jail. This is the real America, right here, among the tractor-trailers without any heat and the tractor-trailers with satellite TV and Internet and the cowboy books on CD and the heavy metal mixtapes and however many milligrams of speed or cocaine or meth or whatever combination thereof it takes to keep you going 48, 54, 72 hours, although not on your runs, buddy, not for the hauls you call in, all that drug shit's in the past and maybe the future too, you know how life is.

For a while my brother stops calling so often, and I worry he's sinking into some dark hole he can't get out of, all those long hours of guitar practice upstairs in his bedroom all through junior high and high school, and all those hours, days, weeks, months, years, by now almost a decade cramped in shitty band vans, logging miles, losing sleep, playing shows for thirteen or thirteen thousand, all of it wasted now, and him locked into some blue-collar management slave life not unlike what we watched our dad do all those years among air-conditioning men and sheet-metal men before he went back to college and clawed and scratched his way up to the corporate life, the desk and the dictaphone. My brother calls and says that's the kind of thing that sounds good to him now, the desk and the secretary and the screaming boss and the health insurance plan, HMO or PPO, I care not which. I want to go home, he says, and watch TV and chop vegetables like Emeril Lagasse and melt butter and sprinkle garlic on top. I want to mow the lawn and take my dog outside to walk and lift his leg by the neighbor's mailbox. I want to paint the walls whatever color I want and go to the Baptist church and find some saved bad girl who wants to be monogamous and watch Scooby Doo and laugh at my corny jokes and get married and cook me dinner and take vacations to the Magic Kingdom or Epcot Center and ride the monorail from the Contemporary Hotel to the Polynesian Village. To me it all sounds terrible, and I tell him so. I tell him he was the reason I became a fiction writer and stopped being a preacher and stopped believing in God. I tell him he was the reason I was able to quit home and quit life and make a new life for myself based upon an idea of myself as a new kind of person I could invent and become, and I was able to do it because he did it first. "When you quit school," I say, "and moved to Nashville and dyed your hair blue and started wearing eye makeup, I looked around me and said, What's keeping me here? and the answer was nothing was. The only thing keeping me from becoming me was me. Me listening to what everybody else said life had to be, and me trying to believe what everybody else said I was supposed to believe, and me being somebody that other people could get behind. Just me. And that would still be me if it wasn't for you doing what you did."

It sounds ridiculous coming out of my mouth, and even if I could find a way to believe it wasn't so, he tells me. "What you're saying is childish," he says. "It's ridiculous. There's no life in music or stories or art or whatever. Everything takes money. Everybody needs health insurance. I'm tired of not having money. I'm tired of being poor. If people are going to treat me like dogshit, I want to get money for it. I want to get paid. I don't want to be afraid I'm going to lose my house. I don't want people's parents to act like I'm some kind of lazy person when I work harder than anybody I know. I want to wear khaki pants. I want to sit at a desk. I want to go to meetings." This uprightness lasts another week or so. Then somebody calls from California. They need a bass player who can sing background vocals, road manage, and look good under the stage lights. Three hundred bucks a night and they leave for Ontario tomorrow. "Sign me up," my brother says, and gives a few hours' notice.

My father calls me, sick with the news. "That trucking company was a good thing," he says. "Your brother could make a good life with a company like that. You learn those skills, not many people have those skills. The trucking industry is what keeps this whole country afloat. The whole economy. All of it is dependent on those trucks. He's pissing it all away." Uh-huh, I say, and mean it. He is right, my father, and he is almost always right, and soon indeed this new thing will end badly the way all the other things end badly. But I want to say that everything ends badly. Don't we all of us live under the shadow of death, that end of all ends, and isn't life too short to give fourteen hours a day to a trucking company when you could be standing under stage lights making somebody you never met before feel something? What's khaki pants and health insurance compared to that? All night I stay up thinking about it. My child stirs in his sleep in the next room, and I hear some ghostly echo of my brother's voice calling me childish. Sometime the next morning an airplane flies over our house in the direction of Canada, and I wish my brother Godspeed to Ontario.

4.

Another death, and another and another. A college mate from Indiana, a girl, gets on the back of a motorcycle at a party. The driver is a seminarian. When they left the party together, they were laughing. At some residential intersection, a newly licensed sixteen-year-old runs a stop sign and hits them broadside. She flies through the air. He impales his lower body on the bike handle. Her heart stops as she hits the ground forty feet away. His legs are broken and his scrotum ripped open. She dies. He walks with a cane.

Another. In Florida, a meter reader, my friend when I was a preacher. He marries a woman, develops leukemia, she leaves him, he dies. In Indiana, a vagrant crawls into the dumpster where I used to throw my trash as an undergraduate. The garbage truck picks up the dumpster in the morning with its mechanical arms and empties its contents into the back of the truck. The sanitation worker pulls the compactor lever, and the man is crushed to death. The lone African-American professor at the seminary holds a memorial service for the vagrant, and hundreds gather to validate the significance of his life.

In Florida, my uncle Jerry visits my parents' house with his new girlfriend. They make noises like they might get married. She doesn't seem to mind that he is twenty years brain-damaged from his own accident with a city garbage truck. She doesn't seem to mind that he still complains every few hours about losing the love of his ex-wife and his children. She seems to love him. She flashes a ring. He's bought a house. She has a jewelry business. They've bought a commercial building. Everyone hugs goodbye. My uncle and his girlfriend drive home, four hours north. My father says everything's going to be all right now. They're going to be all right.

The next evening my uncle locks himself in his bedroom. He puts his head on his pillow. He puts a pistol in his mouth and pulls the trigger. She knocks on the front door the next morning. She knocks but no one answers. She knocks and bangs and yells. She kicks at the door. She breaks down the door. She finds him weirdly white, a hole in his head, a pool of blood beneath the bed, whatever wasn't soaked up by the mattress as it drained from the hole in his head. My parents drive up. Some people from my uncle's rural church arrive to help clean the bedroom. They carry the blood-soaked mattress outside. My father goes into the bedroom to clean the blood and brains from the wall and the floor, but he cannot. Other men go inside to do the job, but they cannot. In the end a tiny middle-aged woman from the church takes a mop and some rags and a bucket full of water and bleach, and in the end, she scrubs most of it by hand.

I'm there with my parents and the woman who would have been the widow but who was not the widow, through the initial grieving, through the funeral, another funeral, and my father says surely this is as bad as life could possibly be, surely this is the last of the funerals for a while, it better be, we have to take care of each other.

He calls my brother on the phone so many times that my brother stops answering when he calls, and then he worries what it means that my brother won't answer the phone when he calls. I call, and my brother answers, and he says he's off the gig from California, he's not getting paid, keep it to yourself for now. The rich bandleader won't return my brother's phone calls. He emails to say my brother has to deal with his business manager. My father runs down the business manager on the phone in California and quotes the labor statutes and threatens all means of legal and public relations related remedies, and the business manager says she's not going to deal with somebody's father, and my father says the rich bandleader gets a business manager, doesn't he?, well then my son has a business manager, too, and you're talking to him, and then he gets a corporate real-estate attorney writing letters just to be more threatening, and the bandleader's business manager quits, and my brother gets paid, and this rich bandleader who hired him with such urgency and dismissed him so casually tells my brother he has intimidated the business manager unnecessarily, and that he is taking food from the mouths of the bandleader's children, and my father feels better at all this news. See?, my father says, it's getting better. This season of death and despair is over, and we can get back to the business of taking care of each other, and that's what we have to do in this world, take care of each other.

A skinny black cat, a stray, moves into our garage, and my wife begins to feed it. At night, the cat prowls. We hear her at night with the neighborhood tomcats, and soon she is pregnant, and my wife feeds it and feeds it, and the cat grows fat and less weary and lets my wife pet it. Our own baby cries all the time. The cat gives birth to three babies in our garage. One day I have our baby by myself all morning, and all morning he will not stop crying. They used to call this condition colic, but colic seems too benign a word for what this constant crying does to the nervous system of an adult. The only thing that will quiet him is to put him in the car and drive him around town until he stops crying. In a state of agitation, I take him outside and put him in the car seat and start the car as quickly as I can and back out the driveway, but something doesn't feel right, some little wobble on the driver's side. I stop the car and open the door. One of the baby kittens is crushed under the front wheel on the driver's side. It is still alive and mewling. One robin-blue eye is popped from its socket. The other kittens come toward the crushed kitten. The kittens are crying. My baby is crying. The mother cat arrives from the woods where she was foraging. The mother cat is crying. I want to move the car off the dying kitten, but I am afraid I will crush more kittens. Nobody has punched me in the kidneys, but that is what it feels like in my back. I'm doubled over, smelling the kitten. I vomit in the grass. There is a pressure in my sinuses. The mother cat is licking the dying kitten, pushing at its head, pushing its eyeball back toward the socket too crushed to hold it. Cultivated people manufacture their own words for moments—right?—but all I hear is a buzzing, and in my mouth the taste of pennies triggers the sense memory of Ralph Stanley's voice singing "O Death," and there's the smell of amniotic fluid somehow and something in the muscles at the back of my arms and legs like when bigger boys used to beat me in the locker room with those puke-green walls when I was twelve, except now I'm responsible for the baby crying in my car, and I'm responsible for this kitten now dead under the wheel of my car.

I call my wife, and she is in a meeting, and sends her assistant, who brings me a Coca-Cola and offers to move the car and offers to move the dead kitten. All afternoon, the mother cat stands over the dead kitten. When my wife gets home, she feeds our baby. Then she takes a shovel and buries the dead kitten. For three days afterward, the mother cat stands over the place where the kitten is buried and paws at the ground and cries for it. She hides her other kittens in the wooded lot by our garage and doesn't let us see them anymore. She takes our food, but only when we are not around to see her take it. She gets skinny again.

The phone rings. Kentucky. My wife's nineteen-year-old nephew. His mother and father have separated. He's with his father in the ramshackle house in the middle of the Daniel Boone National Forest. He has locked himself in his room and won't come out. He has ingested nothing but Jack Daniels for three days. He is prostrate confessing his sins to God. He has been found passed out, dehydrated. He has been taken to the hospital. The phone rings. The boy again. He has been taken to Arizona. Some kind of cult deprogramming facility where they cast out demons. The phone rings. He has escaped the facility by foot. He has been found under an overpass, dehydrated. The facility won't keep him if he doesn't want to stay. The demons haven't been successfully cast out. They're sending him home to his father and the ramshackle house. The phone rings. The boy's father was in the shower. He didn't hear the boy go out. The boy went up into the clearing on the hill with the shotgun. He put the shotgun in his mouth and he pulled the trigger. He took one of his drums up there with him. They found his body up there with the cracked drum skin. "Would you please tell your wife?"

I tell my wife. We pack our things and drive straight to Kentucky. At the funeral service, the preacher mixes together the bitter ingredients that make sweet biscuits, then eats a biscuit, and says the sweet life is made of bitter parts.

There is an argument about flowers after the service. The boy's maternal grandmother doesn't want anybody from the boy's father's family to take any of the good flowers home. Blame is in the air, and the smell of biscuits. After the service, we go back to the ramshackle house. The boy's mother's pink piano is missing. The boy's father says he and the boy hauled it out and threw it off the porch and took an axe to the wood. There is some talk about the axe splitting a tension string and the string cutting a stripe the length of a forearm. Inside the house, shellacked wasps have been affixed near the eyes of all the mother's Precious Moments figurines. In the bathroom, the boy's father grinds up methadone pills and snorts them in lines. His pupils are pinpricks. I ask for the bathroom. I feel full of death and want to purge. I shit and wipe and throw the paper into the toilet and the toilet stops up. The boy's father comes into the bathroom and says it's all right and plunges the toilet and makes the shit and paper go down. He says it's all right again, then goes outside in his overalls and leans against the building and smokes a cigarette. The bottle of Jack Daniels is in his hand, and I wonder: Is that the bottle? Is that the one the boy took into the bedroom?

In the farmhouse down the gravel road from the ramshackle house, the extended family gathers for what will be the last time, though we don't know it yet, how this fissure was one fissure too many, and so many of us have young families and maybe we don't want to infect one another, and maybe this extended family has become suspect on grounds of infection, although, to me, the taint is on everything, here and everywhere else, too. I ought to be paying attention to my wife. It's her family. But all I can pay attention to is the ratcheting up of the tension inside myself, the grief upon grief upon grief that stacks up so time gets distorted and I can't remember which death came first, or which in what order, not even now while I'm committing these things to paper.

In Kentucky I try to call my brother, but we are in a hollow the cell phone companies haven't valued enough to send a signal. I drive into town to call my brother, but the battery runs out, and none of the local convenience stores sell the right charger. So many times I have called him because I was worried about him, but this is the first time I have called him because I need him to be worried about me. Back at the farmhouse and the ramshackle house, everyone says the same empty words they always say about heaven and God and the way all things work together for good. I have heard them so many times, but now what they mean to me is that life is empty of meaning so people must tell themselves stories about how and in what ways everything means.

These words don't seem to comfort anyone so much, anyway. All the men of my wife's family are outside pushing the lawnmower or building a dam for the creek or whatever kind of physically vigorous thing they can find to do to keep death or the news of death at arm's length, and the children are running around with the dogs, and the women are in the kitchen baking things and cleaning things, and one of them is whistling to ward off silence. That's the only reason I can figure for her whistling.

Night can't come soon enough, and when it does, I beg my wife to drive tomorrow to my brother's house in Nashville. She says let's go now and we'll buy a battery in Lexington and call him from the interstate. We arrive around four in the morning, and he greets us. He is waiting for us. He has known his share of trouble like we have, and now he offers his bedroom. He has drawn the curtains and he has pulled the nightshade. My wife and child lie down in his bed and go to sleep. My brother and me go upstairs to his studio. We throw our bodies onto those beanbag chairs where we've thrown our bodies before, under similar circumstances. There is a documentary on the TV about stone altars in Indonesia, and we watch it with the sound off. The pattern randomizer bounces lines and shapes across a spectrum of bright colors on the monitor beside the TV. All around us, the chalkboard walls and the soundproofing foam and the guitars and the keyboards and all the rack-mounted gear and the computers and the mixing consoles, and next to me, my black bag, with my laptop and my red Cheever book to jump-start language, all the tools with which we're supposed to make meaning or offer pleasure or at least make somebody feel something, but where are we supposed to start finding any of it?

There is nothing but sadness in Nashville, except maybe this one thing we both can say but don't say aloud: My brother loves me, and I love my brother. No more deaths, I don't say. No more suicides. Not me, not you, not anybody we know. No more thefts. No more drugs. No more embezzlements. No more phone calls. No more trouble with women. No more deaths. All night we lie fifteen inches apart on the beanbag chairs and don't say anything at all. I want both of us to be all right. I want all of us to live forever.

FIRST, THE TEETH,

WHITE ENAMEL SET INTO PINK MOLD-INJECTED PLASTIC, set on the table next to the hospital bed, and he says, "Gin"—that's my mom, his daughter—"can you get me some of those white strips?" because he's worried his teeth have yellowed.

At issue is the nurse, the pretty young brunette who has been taking the teeth out, at my grandmother's request, and putting them back in, when she leaves, at my grandfather's request. The old man is shameless as regards the pretty girls. He asks me if I saw the pretty nurse, and I say yes, and he says, "She's right purty," and I agree, and I know he's wishing my little brother was here instead of me, because they have that in common, the eye for the ladies, the dwelling eye.

"He's coming," I say, "in two days. He's flying in from Nashville as soon as he can wrap things up at work."

"Why is he coming?" my grandfather says, and I know right away what he means. He means, *Am I going to die? Is that why you're here, flown to Florida from Ohio?*

"He's coming to see you," I say, and not because we don't both know what's happening, not because I'm humoring him, but because my mother is in the room, and I can't say what he wants

me to say and what I want and don't want to say, which is: *He's coming to see you before you die. He's coming to see you because he loves you,
because he's your favorite and you're his favorite.*

My mother is in the room and she can't bear to hear things like
that. She's not given to much truth-telling, not out loud. She likes to
keep things nice, and for all these years I've thought she was wrong,
but not today. Nobody knows one right thing to say, and neither
does she, but she knows how to stand at the edge of the bed, right
up near her father's head, and touch him, and put her face close to
his. She knows to say, "I forgave you a long time ago," when he says
he's sorry for all the things he's done to her, and she knows not to
make a list, not to catalogue the times he pulled the curtains off the
wall or threw sharp kitchen utensils in drunken rages or let wild
men into the house where his daughters slept at two in the morning. She knows not to mention all the horrible women he met at
honkytonks, or the beatings he gave her older brother and sister, or
the way he made my grandmother so angry she's still trying to get
even, even now, fifteen years after everything got calm and easy for
the first time since they were too young to be married and got married anyway.

"Why is he coming?" my grandfather says, again.

"You can understand what he's saying?" my mother says, to
me.

"Yes," I say.

"It's because he doesn't have his teeth in," my father says. "Bill,
do you want your teeth in?"

He nods his head, says yes.

But no one knows how to put his teeth in. There is a tube of
adhesive by the bed. I think maybe I'll try to put his teeth in. A vol-
unteer summons my parents to the waiting room on the other end of
the floor to consult with the doctor. My mother says I should go get
the nurse, so I leave the room and go looking, but she's somewhere
else, maybe taking a break, or taking someone to the bathroom.

I have my mother's cell phone in my pocket, call my wife in Ohio and tell her about the teeth, and she says, "You have to put them in. You have to just do it."

"I don't know how," I say, and it's true. But it's also true that I don't want to do it. I've been touching him on his chest, and sometimes he's been grabbing my hands, and my face has been so close to his face that I've been taking the full stench of his decaying organs into my nostrils every time he exhales. One time I was walking in the woods and came upon a pile of dead opossums, killed by something bigger and left for some reason I don't know. Every time he exhales I can smell those dead opossums times ten or maybe twenty, a truly noxious odor I don't know anything to do about and can't turn away from out of shame at showing any sort of embarrassment or weakness or, really (to be honest), selfishness.

My wife is not having my protests. "You just put some paste on the plates and stick them up on his gums where teeth go."

"I don't know where to put the paste," I say.

"On the plates," she says.

"I don't know how much," I say. "I don't know where. Two dabs or three? Or spread all around? I don't know. I don't want to mess up his mouth. Or his breathing. He's having trouble breathing."

Every second or third exhalation, a gurgling sound comes from deep in his body. It's so vulgar, but it's what I'm thinking: He's drowning in his own juices.

I see the nurse and know the nurse will save me.

"I found the nurse," I say.

"It's good for you," my wife says. "It's good for all of you to do as much of the physical care for him as you can. Don't just let the nurse do everything."

"Okay," I say, and then I hang up and get the nurse.

He flirts with her when she comes in, and she flirts back, and this flirting has made my mother crazy for as long as I can remember, but now it's a good thing, everyone in the room recognizes it's a good thing. It's a sign of fight, and it's something characteristic, and everything characteristic has become suddenly dear.

The nurse holds up the adhesive tube and asks if it's the right paste, and he says yes, and she fills the dental plate with adhesive, and I can tell by his eyes that it's too much paste, but he doesn't say anything because she's the pretty nurse.

She pushes the upper plate into his mouth, and the paste fills the gap between gum and plate and begins to spill over the sides and out the back of the dentures. Some of it drips down into his throat, and he begins gagging, and the gurgling starts to get worse, and still she keeps pushing the plate against his gums, not stopping until he begins to cough convulsively. Then she yanks the teeth out of his mouth and replaces them with gauze to wipe up the extra paste.

I watch her and wonder how many times she's taken his teeth out and put them back in, and why can't she get it right?

She is apologizing, and my mother and father have left the room to consult with the doctor, and my grandfather is gagging and wheezing and can't respond, so now she is apologizing to me.

"How many times have you done this before?" I ask her.

"It's just there's so many patients," she says. "They all like it different ways. It's hard to keep straight."

She wipes the paste from the plate with fresh gauze, then holds the dentures out to my grandfather and asks him if he'd like to do it.

He reaches for the teeth, and his hands are shaking, but not so violently as they begin to shake when he takes the teeth in his hands.

The teeth must weigh a few ounces, maybe five or six if they're heavy. It is a measure of how weak he is that so little weight registers at all.

He transfers the teeth into his left hand and asks me to squeeze the paste onto the plates. I ask the nurse if she will do it, and he scowls at me, as if to say, *She's the one who screwed it up in the first place.* He lets her do it, though, and she says, "Where?" and he points with one shaking finger to the middle, right behind the front teeth, and says, "Pea-size," but she doesn't understand his words without his teeth in, and I have to translate. "Pea-size," I say.

She tries for pea size, but it's not enough, and he tries to tell her, but the effort sends him into a coughing fit. He drops the teeth, and I have to catch them so they won't fall onto the floor.

It is the first time I have touched the teeth.

I did not want to touch the teeth.

They are cold in my hand, and wet from his mouth, and sticky from the failed attempts to get the paste right.

I look up at his mouth, and he stops coughing and closes his eyes. His breathing is all wrong, starts and stops. His mouth hangs limp and loose like the mouths of many old people I have known, but it is different with my grandfather, because he is my grandfather. It's not right for him to be dying here without his teeth, and I decide that I will finish the job. I will apply the paste and put the teeth into his mouth and stay here beside the bed until he dies to make sure that no one takes them out, or, to be more specific, that my grandmother doesn't come back and tell the nurses to take them out.

But that's not what happens. What happens is my mother and my father walk back into the room and take charge, ask what is taking so long with the teeth. The nurse snaps to attention, and she's suddenly competent, takes the teeth from my hand and expands the drop of paste to pea-size, and then two more, one on each side, half an inch from the last molar.

She presses the teeth into my grandfather's gums, and they stick, and for a few minutes he rallies. He asks if I'm still writing a book about him, and I lie, I say yes, and he knows it's a lie, and I know it's a lie, and it's a lie that pleases him, and I wish for more lies, a hundred lies, a thousand beautiful lies, any ugliness that will nourish him.

IN A DISTANT COUNTRY

I.

Rev. Samuel Tillotson, Baptist Mission, Koulèv-Ville, Haiti, to Mr. Leslie Ratliff, Principal, Good Shepherd Academy, West Palm Beach, Florida, June 11, 1983.

Technically, Leslie, and in keeping with the practice we're supposed to maintain around here, I'm supposed to be writing to thank you for visiting last month with your graduating seniors, and for the gifts toward the 44 cubic ft. refrigerator for the mission and the new stone cistern for the village and especially the ionized oxygen allotrope gas (IAOG) water filtration system, which, I'll admit, this place has badly needed for as long as I can remember. I'm also supposed to make you aware of our other needs, among them the replacement diesel generator, the razor-wire project to replace the broken-glass deterrent atop the mission walls, and 142 sponsorships for our planned expansion of the school-and-food project at the Angels of Mercy orphanage up the road.

In many ways, though, it pains me to make you aware of any of it, or to give you the missionary song and dance at all, really. The best thing about seeing you again was taking those long walks out into the village where we could be candid. Leslie, I'm lonely, and wanting for candidness these days. The mission board is threatening to yank thirteen percent of our funding, which means whoever first talks out of turn in front of someone else gets sent home without so much as a kiss goodbye, so here lately I'm silent as a monk. The Haitians are candid among themselves, but not with me. They look at me and all they see is a walking cash machine, and who could blame them? Good people like you come to visit, and we're not to be candid with you, either, because you're *our* cash machine. We scam people, Leslie. The last two groups before you—the bonnet-heads from Pennsylvania I told you about, and the Alabama rednecks whose minister kept sneaking off with his dip can—Brother Joe told Henri, our driver, to take the good tires off the truck before he picked them up from the airport, and put on the old worn-out set instead. Right there in the airport parking lot, he shows the tires to the group leaders, says, "Times are hard. I hope we make it to the mission on those things." Sure enough, on the way there, both times, one of the tires blows out, and Henri gets out to patch it, and up there in the back of the truck, the group leader is already calculating how much for each tire, and how quickly he can wire the money from the States.

I wouldn't let them do that to you, Leslie. I probably ought not let them do it to anyone at all, but you have to pick your battles. Remember Professor Phelps, our first year at old Apalachicola Bible College, talking equality this and justice that? He was right, and we all knew it, or ought to have known it: They should've been letting blacks into that college all along. But, thinking about it, if Phelps had just kept his mouth shut, say, four more years, history would have caught up to him, because they let the blacks into Apalachicola Bible College eventually anyway, didn't they? But they never let Phelps back in, ever. That's something I think about from time to time, when I'm thinking about opening my mouth. Wise as serpents, harmless as doves, the Scripture says.

Enough griping. Here's the real reason I'm writing you. It's obvious you are running a quality school up there in West Palm Beach. Your students were uniformly well-behaved, and more mature than many of the ones we get from the church groups or even the college groups. I found them to be highly intelligent, cooperative, and given to the highest standards of moral uprightness. No doubt you think of them as children, since you have seen them along their journey since they were children. But to a person like me, meeting them for the first time at the ages of seventeen and, mostly, eighteen, they didn't really seem like children so much as they seemed like the young adults they have become. They have graduated now, Leslie, and you have turned them loose into the world knowing that you've done your job well. It must be hard for you, to turn them loose, but every year you do it, and I imagine it brings you not a little sadness to go along with your hard-earned pride.

One of these students in particular, the young lady named Sheila Brocken, impressed me even more than most. From day one, it was clear that she was not here to pal around with her girlfriends or have a Third World frolic or impress the boys. She was here to touch the lives of others. You should have seen her up there, Leslie, at Angels of Mercy, combing the little girls' hair, braiding it, placing beads. Or upstairs, where they keep the retarded kids, touching their faces, picking them up, spinning them around in circles until they were giddy with laughter.

I'm not the only one who noticed Sheila, either. The day after the field trip to our hospital, one of the nurses came over to see me. You met her, remember? Yvonne, from Gonaïves? Sheila's whole day, Yvonne told me, was spent down in the hospital basement, where we keep the pregnant girls, the ready-to-pop girls who don't have families, or whose families don't have a place for them. Haiti is a grim place for girls like these, Leslie. We can only keep them until the babies arrive, and then they're on their own, and they know it. But this girl of yours, this Sheila, she was only four days in country, and she had already learned the words for *good*, for *beautiful*. All day she was touching their faces, touching their swollen bellies, saying *bon, bel, bon, bel*, and even more than the words was the way she said them, her smile, which—I agree with what Yvonne said—it was like an angel had come down from heaven to lift us all a little closer to it for a little while.

That last day you were here, Leslie, in the morning—I hope you will forgive this small indiscretion—I went to see Sheila before breakfast. My motives were not ulterior, I assure you. It's just that I had observed in her these very special qualities of faith and goodness, and others had observed them in her as well, and I felt it was my duty, as host and representative of the mission, to praise and encourage these qualities, and to let her know, on behalf of the Baptist Mission, how much I appreciated the way she cared for the children and young women under our care.

That's all it was, Leslie. That's all I intended. I asked her to take an early morning walk with me through the village, the same route I walked with you, past the home of Yves and Prudeut Estimee, where we're building the stone cistern, and alongside the fields where the farmers from our co-op are doing their planting, and down the red dirt path toward Fermathe, where she could mingle some with the children walking to school in Pétion-Ville, and the working men making their way toward the paved roads to meet the tap-tap.

Sometime on the way back toward the mission, we passed those fields again, and I told Sheila the same story I told you, about this carpenter Rene who has a co-op plot where he grows cabbage and lettuce. I told her how Rene had a little bit of money in his pocket because he was saving to pour a foundation for a new house. His wife knew about this money and asked him to give her some, because her aunt had died, and she wanted to go to the beauty salon in Pétion-Ville and get her hair and nails done for the funeral. But Rene said no. He was firm. They had a child on the way, and he planned to build her a new house with a floor. He asked her, "Do you want our baby to sleep on dirt?" But his wife was angry anyway, and told all the women in her family that Rene had this money and he was keeping it from her, and many of these women went home and badmouthed Rene to their husbands. The next day, one of these husbands went to see Rene. He said, "I am family. I am the husband of your wife's cousin. I know you have some money in your pocket, and I need work. I am a good roofer. You should hire me to repair your roof." Now, Leslie, it's true that Rene's roof needed mending. It was one of those corrugated aluminum numbers you see all over the village, and the last few storms had loosened its moorings to the top of Rene's tiny old one-room house, the one he had been born in, dirt floor and all. But it's something Rene can fix himself. He needs the money for his foundation, and he's under no obligation to this husband of his wife's cousin. So Rene turns his back politely and replies, "I'm truly sorry, I can't hire you today." At this, the wife's cousin's husband becomes very angry. Later that day, he brings his cow down into Rene's field and lets him loose to graze on Rene's cabbage and Rene's lettuce.

I didn't even yet get to the end of the story, Leslie, where Rene asked me what to do, and I told him to do what the law allows and confiscate the cow and charge the offending man a fee for every day Rene kept him. It's a good story. I had a head of steam, and I wanted to finish it. But all of a sudden I look over at Sheila, and two lines of tears are rolling down her cheeks. She's not crying for attention, she's not making a sound, but the tears are just rolling down her cheeks, and she says, "Brother Samuel, your heart for these people is so beautiful to me."

When she said it, Leslie, I didn't know what to do with it. It was like she reached into my chest and clawed at the scab that had been covering over the wound of my loneliness. I reached both hands to her face, and I wiped the line of tears from each cheek. By then we had been gone too long, so we started the walk back to the mission. She was still crying some, and she leaned into me. I put my arm around her, to comfort her, that's all.

Ever since then, Leslie—ever since I brought her back to the mission in time for breakfast, ever since Henri and I took all of you to the airport, ever since I watched that American Airlines jet light out toward the water, and imagined her trajectory past La Gonave, past the eastern ridge of Cuba, past Turks and Caicos and the Bahamas, and wished her safely all the way toward Miami International— she has been with me, in my thoughts, in my prayers. Forgive me this detail, but I can still smell her apple shampoo on the shirt I was wearing when she leaned against me as we walked together toward the mission.

It is a risk to tell you these things, Leslie. I don't have to tell you it is a risk. To a certain kind of person it might seem the slightest bit unseemly, a man of forty-two so taken with a young woman only eighteen years old, and that after only a week together. But you know me, Leslie. We are bosom friends and have been ever since we shared Room 23F in the Oldham-Betts dormitory at Apalachicola. And you know, too, that my life has borne out again and again how God's ways are not our own. I never planned to come to this place any more than I had planned to attend Bible College in my thirties. You've heard me preach plenty of times about how I was engaged to be married to Marisa Holden, how I had a thriving plumbing business with my brother Frank, how I had a whole happy life planned out in High Springs—good honest work Monday through Friday, dinner every evening with Marisa, six or seven kids, at least one of them a boy I was going to name Samuel Jr., weekends out at the cold springs, jumping off those cliffs, swimming in those shallow caves, picnic blankets, cold cuts, laying out there in the cool of the evening with Marisa and the kids. . . .

But the Lord got ahold of me, Leslie, in a tent meeting of all places. They don't even have tent meetings in High Springs anymore. This might for all I know have been the last of the tent meetings. And that preacher laid his hands on my head and said, "The Lord is commissioning you to bring the good news to a faraway place," and I already knew it before he said it. Do you think it was easy, Leslie, to walk away from Marisa? To walk away from my business? To walk away from my brother? I didn't understand it at the time, but I had faith. I had trust. I believed in the things I had not seen, and it led me to Apalachicola, to Room 23F in the Oldham-Betts dormitory, to you, to the mission board, and eventually here, to Koulèv-Ville, Haiti. My home, Leslie.

What I'm trying to say is that God works in mysterious ways, which is a thing we all say but we hardly ever believe enough to let it happen to us. I'll admit, even here, even after everything I've seen and done since that tent meeting, even I am reluctant sometimes to do the strange things a person might have to do if that person is open to the word of the Lord. But, Leslie, here's what I'm trying to tell you, strange as you and me might find it to be, strange as it certainly is: When I was walking that dirt path with Sheila Brocken, I wasn't thinking for once about what all things I had given up for the Lord's work. I wasn't thinking about my loneliness. I wasn't thinking about my past or my present, not about the mission board or the thirteen percent budget cut or money this or that. Leslie, I wasn't even thinking how she was eighteen and I was forty-two. All I was doing was just being present in the moment, being open to the Lord and all he has for us, and in that moment what I was hearing—clear as day—was the word from the Lord: This young woman, this Sheila Brocken, is the one I've been keeping aside for you. This young woman, this Sheila Brocken, is the one I've had you waiting for.

I'll tell you, Leslie, as you know from your own experience in the world of men and women, that this waiting has not been easy for me. Often it has been very difficult. Over the years, before Marisa and especially after, I've had a lot of chances to stray from the promises I've made to the Lord. I may not be the most handsome man in the world, Leslie, but I can't say I've not had my share of admirers. I am a man like you and like every other man, and I can't say I've not been tempted. But here's something I have going for me: I've kept my promises, Leslie. I can stand and proudly say that I've kept myself pure unto the Lord for such a day as today, a day when I can sure enough sit down and write you a letter to say that my history is true, my intentions are pure, my motives are noble, and when I say that I mean to pursue Sheila Brocken, what I mean to pursue is a lifelong kind of love, the honor and cherish kind, the in sickness and in health forsaking all others as long as you both shall live kind.

So what I'm asking, Leslie, is this: You know me. We go back many years. At one time you even said you considered me like an older brother to you. So in that spirit of love and family, I'm asking you to go to Sheila Brocken's father and tell him about me and what I have written you today. Explain to him that even though the circumstances are a little unusual, what with the geographic distance, the difference in age and everything, that this is a situation that seems to be coming from a source more powerful than our human minds can even contemplate, and that we all need to sit down here and try to listen to what God is telling us about his will for me and Sheila. And tell him he should listen to his daughter, too. It might be that I'm a fallible soul. I know I can be. I know I am. So we should see if Sheila is hearing the same thing from the Lord that I think I am hearing. And if it is so, that would seem to me to be a confirmation. We may not understand it, Leslie. Not you or me or Sheila's father or Sheila herself. But it might be right, and we'd be wrong to miss it.

II.

Rev. Joseph B. Waddell, Director, Baptist Mission, Koulèv-Ville, Haiti, to Rev. Ervin Medlock, Caribbean Region Director, Foreign Mission Board, Richmond, Virginia, February 11, 1984.

I'm writing to thank you for your letter dated January 4, and for the good news about the record-breaking Lottie Moon Christmas Offering for Missions. Whatever y'all are doing up there in Virginia, the word must be getting out to the local congregations. I'm proud as punch, because we could sure use some help down here. You'll see I've attached some documentation about some of the building programs we really need to initiate by March or April at the latest to accommodate the swelling need. There are other kinds of capital investments I've noted in those pages, too, chiefly our need for a second diesel generator and a couple of new trucks to facilitate the new outreach work we're doing farther up into the mountains. Our first large-scale project up there involves clothes-washing and bathing stations that collect and concentrate the flow from various mountain springs, so that we can (1) help the people use more of the water from the sources they already exploit, (2) create sanitary barriers between the water people are collecting to drink and the water they are using for bathing and washing clothes, and (3) regularly test the water for various nasties that are making people ill or killing them. The government in Port-au-Prince is very high on the project, and once we get one up and running, if they see that it works, they have agreed to match our funds for the next five. This kind of goodwill is hard-earned. It is evidence of real divinely inspired progress with the temporal powers that be. For all of these things, we are truly thankful.

It is also my burden to keep you up to date about a staffing and spiritual life difficulty about which we have previously corresponded, that being the continuing saga of Brother Samuel

Tillotson. For the sake of clarity, and for whatever records you might want to keep, let me catch you up again. Last May, we had the pleasure of a visit from a group of high school seniors from South Florida, whose job it was to do various camps to encourage our children and infirm, and, in the case of the able-bodied young men, to do some light maintenance around the mission. It was noticed by many staffers that Brother Tillotson, age 42, was spending an unusual amount of time around some of the young girls, particularly one by the name of Sheila Brocken. He and she were seen standing abnormally close at evening devotions, speaking idly in the lunch line, and—this unconfirmed rumor came to us thirdhand, and Brother Tillotson, when confronted, denied it— holding hands in the darkness beneath the mango trees that line three sides of our modest hospital.

None of these observations or whisperings alone would suffice to call Brother Tillotson's reputation into question, but taken together, they certainly raised suspicion enough to invite a confrontation. We followed the Scriptural pattern. First, I went to Brother Tillotson alone and asked him about the talk that had come my way. He admitted to what he called a "brotherly affection" for the young girl, and pointed out that there was nothing inappropriate about friendships between brothers and sisters in Christ. Furthermore, he reminded me that the girl was eighteen years of age, and therefore an adult, not a child. He said that he had done nothing to violate Scripture, doctrine, or conscience, and that he resented my questioning.

I'll admit that I went to see him in a spirit of distress. I was worried, frankly, about appearances. The school group that had visited included children from many of the families in the Palm Lake Baptist Association, a group of forty churches of which at least thirteen give directly to our mission in excess of the support they already offer the Foreign Mission Board. I fully expected Brother Tillotson to admit that he had been in some small ways inappropriate, for the two of us to make our peace with what had been, and agree to forge on anew. But his belligerence caught me unawares, and in my surprise, I did not summon up wisdom enough to recall for him the words of Paul to the Corinthians: "Wherefore, if meat causeth my brother to stumble, I will eat no flesh for evermore, that I cause not my brother to stumble."

So I went to see Brother Tillotson a second time, and I took with me Brother Johnson and Brother Garvey. We confronted him again with what we had heard. Brother Garvey, in his gentle way, said, "Samuel, we come in a spirit of love. We're not here to judge you. We're imperfect people just like you. We're not even saying you did anything wrong. We're just asking you to think about avoiding the very appearance of evil, for the good of this whole place."

I'll tell you what, Ervin. Brother Tillotson was unmoved. If it had been anybody else besides this dear brother, I would have had his bags packed and shipped to the airport with him and his one-way ticket before you could say boo. But even with all this, I figured you have to give the man the benefit of the doubt. Up until then, he had been a model citizen, a good fundraiser, good with mechanical projects and good with people and a good administrator of the farm co-op program which has been such a success for us here. So instead of doing what I should have done, and taking him before the whole body, I just pulled him aside. I'm not ashamed to tell you what I told him. I reminded him about the thirteen percent budget reduction we were facing. I reminded him of my discretion under these circumstances. I said, "You're on thin ice, buddy." I said, "I'm telling you this for your own good and the good of this mission. You pull any more stunts with anymore visiting girls and you're out on your ear." He nodded and hung his head and thanked me and said all right. It seemed to me like I had got through to him, like maybe what we had was just a bout of the single man's blues, something even an old married chump like myself could understand. The end. Case closed. Problem solved. Or so I thought.

Last September 3, Brother Tillotson asked for and was granted a two-week furlough. His stated reason was "private family matters back home." Upon his return, I personally went to the airport to pick him up, and, to my surprise, found that he was traveling with the young girl from the school group, Sheila Brocken. She was wearing a thin bright orange dress that only covered her legs to mid-thigh, orange boots, and large earrings shaped like hula hoops. They were holding hands, and he was grinning like the cat that ate the bird. Things being so sideways, I didn't know how to even address him directly, so I said, "Brother Samuel, when I took you to the airport you boarded with one carry-on bag, and now I see you have six suitcases." Big suitcases, mind you. Two big green matching hardshell cases like were popular when I first came over here myself, and one pink and one powder blue, and two smaller soft-sided bags. Brother Tillotson lifted up the hand of Sheila's he was holding and pushed it toward me and said, "Meet Madame Samuel," and I'll admit the quarter-carat on her finger seemed to me flawless in color, cut, and clarity. I asked him who performed this ceremony, and he produced and unfolded a paper from his pants pocket, attested by the Clerk of the Circuit Court, witnessed by Frank Tillotson and Robert Tillotson (do these last names ring familiar to you as they did to me?), and stamped and sealed by all due civil authorities in Alachua County, Florida.

I'm sure it was quite a sight, the three of us parading those suitcases through the mission. You should have seen all the extraneous material in those suitcases. Blowdryers, curling irons, hot rollers, makeup boxes, all varieties of shoes, cassette tape players and headphones, all manners of shoes and clothing, dolls and stuffed animals, books and magazines, a small record player and stereo system, bubble-wrapped record albums, colored pens and pencils and drawing papers, feminine sundries, boxes of Little Debbie snack cakes, a typewriter, postage stamps and envelopes, rolled wall posters, a snorkel and fins set.

I pulled Brother Tillotson aside and asked him if he had given any thought to the matter of where Sheila would be housed, much less where her things would be housed. "My room," he said, not having given a moment's thought, obviously, to the notion that perhaps his room was too small to house a larger bed, too spartan to house a woman, too full already to accommodate all the possessions she had seen fit to bring. "It's not as though she overpacked for a holiday," Brother Tillotson explained to me. "She's come here to make a home."

How, Ervin, could I spell it out for him? How could I help him come to terms with the deep and abiding nature of his selfishness? Surely this girl had not undergone a period of preparation for living in a country such as ours, with all its hardships. Surely he had not considered the strain upon our facilities and resources which she now represented. Surely we had not been party or even privy to the decision-making process by which he had imposed her upon us.

Immediately and right away, the other women began to complain about her. Sheila in her vanity was burning the available electricity early, every day, running her hair dryers and her curling irons. Sheila was running around in shorts rather than dresses, her bare long legs hanging out in contravention of the long tradition of women in this place. Sheila was out in the village with the boys and their drums, teaching them American rock and roll songs instead of hymns, or doing the hymns themselves as though they were American rock and roll songs. Sheila's French was abysmal, and instead of bringing it up to speed, she was privileging the local Creole she was learning out in the village, and in so doing, setting an example that would keep the lower classes low, in contravention again of our long practice. On Sunday mornings, Sheila was overdoing it with the lipstick and the eyeshadow, overdoing it with the brightly colored dresses, making a show of herself that made the other women feel less desirable themselves, that made them worry that their own husbands' heads would be turned inappropriately, not because their husbands were bad men, but because their husbands were, quite simply, men, and it is the responsibility of a godly woman, they wanted to tell her (and did, repeatedly), to avoid making herself into an unhealthy distraction.

Brother Tillotson, for his part, was not strongly receptive to various kinds of advice and wise counsel offered for his benefit by others on our staff. To the contrary, he was full of suggestions for how we might adjust to Sheila, for how we might better understand Sheila, for how we might make Sheila more comfortable. Now, Ervin, I am not suggesting that it is inappropriate for a man to wish to please his beloved, nor am I suggesting that there isn't more we could have done on our part to ease the transition despite its having so caught us by surprise. But many of these suggestions seemed less like suggestions than demands, and they were quite often couched in rather manipulative phrasings that made them difficult to properly deflect. For example, the matter of housing. "I can't help but notice," Brother Tillotson said, "how Brother T.C. and Sister Thelma, or Brother Larry and Sister Patty, are quartered in large bedrooms with large beds, attached to private bathrooms, while me and Sheila are still in a tiny outer room where we have to walk to single-sex community showers with the staff members who are single. Haven't I been here longer than any of them? Don't I outrank them? For me, I don't mind, but now I have a family to think about. I have Sheila to think about."

This argument extended to his stipend. It is true that single staffers are paid fairly less than married staffers, and that a married man must think about putting money away for his eventual return to the States. But when we evaluate staff members for our mission, we evaluate them as single or married people, and make our choices taking into account their own character and the character of their spouses, and the resulting financial need, with an eye toward our own budget. Certainly we would expect that some of our single staff members would one day want to marry, but we would expect a reasonable time of waiting, and a conversation within our community about the marriage. That way, we could help prepare the couple for marriage, offer wise counsel to the intendeds, make budgetary and housing arrangements for the year forthcoming. I'll admit, Ervin, to losing my patience with Brother Tillotson after one of these conversations. I'll admit to speaking to his selfishness, dragging that girl down here. "But now, friend," I told him, "what's done is done." I said we would revisit the salary issues at the annual board meeting, but for now we could move the Haitian maids out of the housekeeping suite and move him and Sheila into their place.

Mind you, Ervin, this room moving was quite the undertaking. I would estimate I personally lost three days of mission work accomplishing it. The maids were understandably upset to be so uprooted, and, strangely, they bore no ill will toward Sheila or Brother Tillotson, but reserved all of it for me, the decision maker. They were afraid we would move them out to the village, which perhaps we should have done, because they had grown unnecessarily fat in the comfort of the mission. Instead, Brother Tillotson, Brother Johnson, and I refurbished six storage areas, which, with the room the Tillotsons had abandoned, provided seven single-occupant rooms for the maids. We expanded the women's shower from three nozzles to five, and my Junie even made new cloth privacy curtains to replace the old ones, which had grown rather moldy and raggedy. Brother Tillotson negotiated a price with a man who had some wooded property up the mountain a ways, chopped down eight pine trees, hauled them to a warehouser in Pétion-Ville, traded them for the cured cedar boards Sheila coveted, and fashioned by hand a new queen size canopied bed for his and Sheila's new room, with matching nightstands and a five-drawer dresser. For all the concerns I have about Brother Tillotson, his woodwork is not one of them. Ervin, the only word I can use to describe this bed is decadent—sheer lines, intricate woodcuts up and down the four posters—the whole thing done without benefit of table saw, belt sander, lathe, or router. It cost Brother Tillotson three weeks of evenings in his own labor. When he was done, he drove down to the shop in Port where Michèle Duvalier herself buys bedroom furniture, somehow established a line of credit, and returned with a queen size mattress, bedsprings, black silk bedskirts, and a garish silk canopy, the color a deep garnet fit for the Queen of Sheba.

I did not and will not begrudge a man nice things, especially nice things made nice by the sweat of a man's own brow. The problem with the bed was not its luxury. The problem with the bed was the noises that came from it, night after night, often late into the night, disturbing the sleep of other men's wives, causing troublesome questions child to parent. An informal council of married men was convened, not out of secrecy or malice or any other ill motive, but in order to come to a decision about how to handle the matter of the bed and the noise quietly and delicately, with a minimum of embarrassment to either of the offending parties. After much prayer and discussion, we decided that the wise course of action would be to invite Brother Tillotson into our meeting that very day, and confront him directly about the noise, to say, as married men ourselves, we understood the prerogatives of the newly wedded, and that we were not people who bought into the idea that God is some kind of cosmic killjoy, that we knew full well that the pleasures of the marriage bed are God-ordained, and that he and his bride had our blessing on their goings-on, not that our blessing was necessary. But that we requested—out of courtesy, out of decency—that they keep it down in there, bearing in mind that the designers of the mission had been strategic in placing the old housekeepers' quarters quite centrally, so that the maids could have quick and efficient access to the beds they were expected to make daily, and that the unforeseen placement of the Tillotsons in the housekeeping suite had the unexpected side-effect of making efficient the broadcasting of the noises coming from inside.

So we sent for Brother Tillotson. But when he arrived, he arrived with Sheila. His posture was quite defensive—his body drawn up to its full six feet, four inches, and his arms protectively around her shoulders—and he said, "If you have anything to say, you can say it to both of us. We are man and wife. We are a unit. We are a team. We won't be divided and conquered," and went on this way for quite a long time, with plenty of pious talk about two becoming one flesh and so on, and on, and on. I don't know about the other men, but watching him hold forth, seeing the gray in his hair, seeing his size alongside her tininess, I was struck (perhaps unfairly) with the idea that what we were facing here was not much more than a young and immature girl unfairly saddled to a man closer to pasture than he could imagine, and I was ashamed and unwilling to discuss such a thing as their noise in her presence. Perhaps you, Ervin, are a man more worldly than I am or than any of the other men in that room were or are, but my suspicion is that you would have been taken with these kinds of thoughts yourself, and my shame extended outward, and expanded until it took unto itself the shame that they themselves ought to be feeling for shacking up, but which they clearly did not feel, since they were holding forth daily in postures of such pride.

My thinking about these matters has become bothersome to my own spirit. Ervin, how does a person even begin to address such shame, since it cannot be undone without entering into grave sin— what God has joined together let no man tear asunder, and all that? In the weeks that have followed, Brother Tillotson has rejected every attempted pulling-aside to discuss the matter, holding to his line that his marriage is not a subject for addressing to anyone except both parties, together, and rejecting the rejoinder that his duty as the man and therefore the head of the household is to be the representative of the household in matters that ought not be discussed in mixed company. Meantime, Brother Tillotson continues to minister to the co-op farmers, teach them how better to cultivate their vegetables, raise their rabbits, tend their fish ponds, negotiate with buyers and sellers, and invest their earnings in their own homesteads for the purpose of building a future for their families. He prays with them, trains their leaders, travels with their leaders to seed other villages with the tree of civilized life, and all of it toward the ends we are all of us pursuing—the glory of God and the promotion of His eternal Kingdom. It is as though there are two Brother Tillotsons—the one who has made family of strangers, and the one who has no time or patience for the granting of simple human dignity with the true family of neighbors and friends he lives among here at the mission. Part of me is inclined to stay silent and grant to Brother Tillotson the great grace that bears witness to the grace God offers us all. But part of me is weary, partly from my heart for those who are hurting here in Haiti, partly because neighborly peace has been breached here in the mission, partly because of my growing concern for the blind spots in Brother Tillotson's own character, partly because of my worry for the girl Sheila, and partly quite frankly from the absence of the silence we all need in order to rest properly at night, because, Ervin, the noises continue.

III.

Rev. T. C. Johnson, Baptist Mission, Koulèv-Ville, Haiti, to Rev. Ervin Medlock, Caribbean Region Director, Foreign Mission Board, Richmond, Virginia, February 10, 1986.

I'm sure news of the regime change is getting to you in dribs and drabs, and I send this dispatch with fervent prayers that it will be received. My first obligation is to report whether or not the mis-

sion has weathered the change in government safely. I'm sorry
that I don't know any other way to be but direct. It is my devasta-
tion, telling you that the Lord has taken Brother Joe Waddell and
Brother Sam Tillotson to be with Himself in this hour. It was me and
Brother Larry Garvey who found their bodies. It is no comfort to
me that they passed while engaged in acts of service (trying to save
the water station). We buried them this evening beneath the mango
trees behind the hospital. I pray the circumstances surrounding
their passings might be comfort to their families as time passes, but
to me it is nothing but sheer agony to write you and tell you about
it. Our good Henri is at the gate waiting to courier this letter to the
MFI pilot in Port, and time is short. I will try to write more this evening, but I do not know when I will next have an opportunity to get
an envelope out. Please pray for us.

Rev. Larry Garvey, Jr., Baptist Mission, Koulèv-Ville, Haiti, to Rev.
Larry Garvey, Sr., University Baptist Church, Jacksonville, Florida,
February 13, 1986.

The first thing we saw was the black smoke. Not the thin reeds of
cooking smoke that rise throughout the village, but a thick, wide
swath of smoke. Then voices arguing loudly. Then much shout-
ing. Sam came running in from the village and said, "It's started."
Brother Joe told us to close the mission gates. We had trouble closing them because someone drove an old pickup truck in front of one
of them and started a small fire in the truck bed and left it there. We
had to put out the fire, and we had to move the truck. Some of the
maids and some of the drivers and some of the doctors and nurses
from the hospital helped. We all helped. People began to throw
rocks, seeing us close the gates. Others were trying to get inside.
Sam wanted to let certain ones of them in. Brother Joe said no. They
argued. Brother Joe pulled rank. Sam cursed at him.

By then, the women were running out of the mission buildings to see about the commotion. Brother Joe told them to go back inside. Sam said men were burning tires out by the road. We heard pistol shots. Sam said there were men in the village who knew how to make Molotov cocktails. He worried the mission would be a target. Brother Joe said the people would be with us because of our good reputation for taking care of them. Sam called him naïve. Everyone knew it was us who had built the new water station. The rumor in the village was that we had taken money from the government to build it. Brother Joe said that wasn't true and the people in the village knew it wasn't true. Sam said some people were saying Macoutes had delivered us the money in burlap sacks.

I've never once so much as thought about disrespecting Brother Joe's leadership. But who knows the talk in the village better than Sam? T. C. and I urged Brother Joe to listen to Sam. Brother Joe said it didn't matter if Sam was right or not. All we could do now was hunker down, turn off the generators, get the doctors and nurses locked safely in the hospital, get the other workers into the buildings, get the women and the children as far from the gates and the walls as possible, and pray. Sam said we should take all the extra food we had—all the hundred-pound bags of rice, all the vegetables, all the salted meats, all the boxed provisions—and set it outside the gate. Sam said he would go out there himself and tell everyone it was theirs to take, a celebration gift.

Brother Joe was very concerned about giving away the food. "The precedent," he said. He forbid it. Like always, there was a standoff. Brother Joe must have thought T. C. and me would follow orders like always. But this wasn't like always. This was an extraordinary circumstance if there ever was one. I looked at T. C., and T. C. looked at me. We decided that way. T. C. said, "Sam, let's go on in there and start hauling that food out."

Brother Joe gave me a Judas Iscariot look the way he can. He said, "Are you gonna forsake me, too?"

I said, "I'm not forsaking anybody, Brother Joe." Then I followed Sam and T. C. into the storehouse and started hauling food.

Brother Joe stood there and watched us with his arms crossed. At first he looked angry, but then he looked scared. His foot was tapping. I felt for him. Real softly, I touched his shoulder. I said, "Brother Joe, we really need your help right now."

He kind of dropped his gaze and went into the storehouse and came back out half-dragging a hundred-pound bag of rice. He helped us and didn't complain anymore. The four of us hauled all that food out by the gate. Then Sam climbed up so his head was sticking up over the gates. He started calling names. Pierre, Carlo, Kenel, Michel, Victor. I did not see any of them standing nearby, but they were friends. Sam knew they would be watching over us. They came from the places where they were hiding, and told the other people near the gates to stand aside. Sam told them about the food. He said it was a gift to the village to celebrate the flight of the Duvalier family from the country. He said we were going to open the gate, and would the people stand back so we could bring the food outside?

Pierre and Kenel began to yell orders to everyone to stand aside, and because they are such big men and so respected in the village, people backed away as they approached. Sam came down from the wall, and he said, "Move fast, because there's gonna be a crush."

We opened the gate to about three feet wide. Pierre and Kenel stood guard at the threshold. Sam, Joe, T. C., and I lifted, carried, and dragged the various bags and boxes of food outside. Right away the people began to press in on us, to get at the food. Carlo, Michel, and Victor called for orderliness. Pierre and Kenel crossed their arms. At first, that was enough to slow the press, but now people were coming from all over the village. Others came from the direction of the road and the smoke. People running, people yelling, people whistling for more people. The noise of it was astounding. "It's too much," Brother Joe said. He was yelling over the din. Sam nodded his assent. I noticed that we were all waiting for Sam's assent. When he nodded, we went back inside the gates. Pierre and Kenel helped hold people off as we closed them.

Plenty of the extra food was still inside the gate. "What now?" Brother Joe said. Now he was looking to Sam, too. It seemed to trouble Sam that Brother Joe was treating him as the leader, even though you would think it was what he had wanted all along. Maybe it wasn't. He said, "Brother Joe, should we haul the rest back into the storehouse? In case somebody peeks over the wall and sees it?"

Brother Joe seemed to expand to full size again in response to Sam's deference. "We don't want them breaching the gates," he said. We hauled it all back into the storehouse. It was probably half what we had hauled out.

Now Kenel was calling out from the other side of the gates. Sam and Brother Joe, both, went running toward him. T. C. saw him running and said, "Would you look at that?" It was strange to see Brother Joe in fast motion, a man his size. We had never seen him at the gates before except to come and go. Now he climbed up alongside Sam, and they poked their heads over the top to speak with Kenel.

By now the noise from the other side was such that we could not hear what they were saying. After a while, they both jumped down and headed toward the residences. Brother Joe went right past us without saying a word, but Sam put a hand on T. C.'s shoulder and mine and said, "Best get on in with your families now." Then he went in, too.

Me and T. C. followed as far as the exterior doors to the residences. T. C. stopped me there. He had something to say. I encouraged him to come out with it. He said, "I keep a .22 in Thelma's personal drawer. I keep it loaded. I love my children."

I don't think at the moment he was worried about the mission board's rules against guns or any such thing. At the moment, I wished I had one, too. T. C. said, "You want, you bring Patty and the kids over, and we'll hunker down together."

I didn't know what to do. "You think," I said, "a little .22 is gonna keep us safe?"

"Nope," T. C. said. He didn't even blink. "Thelma's in there with the kids praying, and I don't know if that will make a difference beyond calming them all down some." He was probably doing the recent missionary death tally, same as me. Luc Preval, in Gonaïves. Ed Reelitz, up in Okap. Ben Miller, in Les Cayes. Salvador Arruza, in Carrefour. Even the natural causes, like the heart attack that took Brother Joe's Junie last fall. The Lord's ways are not our own.

Brother Joe came out again with his canteen on his belt, and saw us and said, "Get on inside."

"You, too," T. C. said.

Sam came outside and said, "Brother Joe, you ready?"

Brother Joe nodded. "You fellas aren't welcome to join us," he said, "but they're up there busting up the water station."

"You think you're gonna stop them?" T. C. said.

"I think we're gonna go up there with Pierre and Kenel and tell them to come get the rest of our extra food," Sam said. "Ya'll better haul it out again."

Brother Joe was nodding, even though he had just told us to get inside. The color was out of his face. I could tell he didn't want to go up to the water station, but he didn't want Sam to go when he himself wouldn't go, either. It was a matter of his own pride working on him, I think.

T. C. tried to let Brother Joe off the hook. "Let Sam go," he said. "Pierre and Kenel will take good care of him. We need you here. All this extra food is too much for me and Larry to haul out alone again."

Brother Joe just shook his head. The two of them walked toward the gates, and then they scaled them together. They disappeared to the other side, their bodies first, then their heads.

T. C. said we better wait a little while to start hauling the food out. It took forty or fifty minutes to walk to the water station, and it seemed risky to leave the food very long in an open sightline of any heads that might raise themselves over the walls. The broken glass on top of the mission walls didn't seem much a deterrent anymore. I went inside and got Patty and the kids and we went over to T. C.'s and brought some blankets and spread them out on the floor and we all lay down on them and stayed real still.

By then it was starting to get dark. With the generator out and the dark out the windows and all the truly terrifying sounds—the vodou drums unsettling, but the familiar uses of the human voice-box worse—it was all we could do to keep calm. The children, ours and the Johnson's, were preternaturally calm. I feared some kind of shock had taken them. Thelma and Patty prayed in whispers, and T. C. and I spelled them here and there, just to keep soothing voices in play. Every once in a while, the orange red of some roaring fire someplace up the mountain flared up high enough to be visible against the dark of the window.

None of us gave thought enough to Sam's wife, Sheila. All that time, she was alone. It was Patty who realized it first. She leaned against me on the blanket on the floor and said, "Oh no, Larry. Sheila."

T. C. overheard and said, "We got to go out and get the food, anyway, Larry."

We went out into the hallway, toward the old housekeeper's suite where she and Sam stayed. She didn't answer when I knocked. T. C. said, "She's scared." I said, "Sheila, honey, it's me and T. C.," and right away regretted talking to her like a child, saying honey. Sam was always hair-trigger sensitive to anybody saying anything to her that made her feel like a child.

But when she came to the door, she looked for all the world like a child. Her face was ashen and tear-streaked, and her hair was disheveled, and she was a girl whose hair was never disheveled, even after whole days spent in the village. I felt the weight of conviction, looking at her, knowing she had been in there alone and afraid all this time. "He's dead, isn't he?" she said.

It was a spooky feeling, hearing words like that coming from her.

"Nobody's dead," T. C. said. He didn't like her, but you couldn't tell it in his voice, not then. His voice was gentle, fatherly. He reached out his arms and took a step toward her. She took a step back and shut the door softly. The wood grazed his fingertips.

A coldness came into us, then. Later, T. C. said it was the conviction of the Spirit resting on us because of how we had neglected Sheila, but I can't shake the superstition I want to shake, which is that it was our spirits knowing Sam and Brother Joe were gone, before our minds could know it. What happened, in any event, was we picked up bags of rice and carried them to the place just inside the gates where we had carried them before. We carried the salted meats and the vegetables, and we carried the boxed provisions. Then we waited. This was the worst of it. We waited and waited, but neither Sam nor Brother Joe returned.

Sometime around dawn, Henri came knocking on the gates, calling for T. C. and me. When we saw his face, we knew. He said we better come help him collect the bodies. All I could think of was that old homeless lady Marie who died last year out in front of Le Dieu de Justice school and we thought she was just sleeping on the steps again, and how crazy old Jean Sitney covered her with his black blanket, and when her people never did come to take the body, he started dancing with it, round and round in circles, until the school-children stopped him by throwing rocks at his arms and body.

T. C. went over to the place by the mission wall where Sam cultivated the sugar cane, and threw up into it. When he was done, he wiped his mouth, and said, "You gonna go tell Sheila, or you want me to?"

It didn't seem right to make him do it. I knocked on her door again, and as soon as she saw my face, she knew. I could tell. Her voice was flat. "Where?" she said, and I told her the water station. She pushed me aside and took off running, flat-out running, past me, past T. C. and Henri, through the gate, and out into the village.

There was no catching her. Maybe Henri could've caught up with her, but maybe he was as soft as we were, spending his days driving that truck instead of walking up and down the hill for water, instead of walking everywhere, the way most people do who don't live in the mission. The only person in the whole place who could've run from here to the water station was Sheila herself, because she was the only one out running around the village all the time.

The three of us didn't say anything to one another. We just started walking. We walked in a triangle, me and T. C. up front, and Henri, watchful, bringing up the rear. We walked through the village, all the way to where the good dirt path ended, up the mountain, and down again, toward the fresh springs where the people washed and bathed.

You could see the water station busted up from far away. It looked like they had come at it with hammers and axes and pieces of wood. Whatever they could get their hands on. Later we found a young tree that had been pulled up by the roots and swung like a baseball bat. And from that distance, already, we could hear Sheila wailing. She did not sound like herself, but her voice was not strange. She sounded like almost any Haitian woman I had ever seen bent over the body of a lost father, a lost husband, a lost baby. Wailing.

We followed her voice to the far end of the water station. She was knee-deep in the stream. Chunks of concrete and scraps of wood and PVC pipe floated around her or lay in the shallows. Her whole body was leaned over what was left of Sam. Her arms were under his shoulders, holding his head out of the water. Her fore-head dipped in and out of the stream. She was shaking with cold. When we came closer, we saw that the left side of Sam's face was completely caved in.

I had to shout to be heard over the sound of the stream, and her wailing. I said, "Where is Brother Joe?" I asked three times, but she did not answer. She may not have known we were there until T. C. came behind her and put his arms around her. Even then, she did not let go of Sam's body. Some ways downstream, I caught sight of Brother Joe bobbing face down among the reeds. I left Sheila with T. C., and waded toward him, to fish him out of the water. His face was caved in, too. Upstream, T. C. was saying, "He's with Jesus, Sheila. He's with Jesus." I don't think I'll ever see a sight like it again, T. C. holding Sheila, Sheila holding Sam's body, the three of them in the water, bobbing amid all that trash.

IV.

Mrs. Linda Reelitz, Okap Baptist Ministries, Cap-Haïtien, to Rev. Ervin Medlock, Caribbean Region Director, Foreign Mission Board, Richmond, Virginia, May 10, 1986.

I'm sorry it has taken so long to get back with you about this Sheila Tillotson affair. MFI is only running every-other-Tuesday flights out of Cap-Haïtien, and those are Palm Beach hops, with Santo Domingo stops midway. So the fastest cheap way into Port-au-Prince is Okap to Santo Domingo on Tuesday morning, then the Thursday afternoon flights to Port with the Presbyterians. On the way back, it was the Presbyterians to Santo Domingo, then (lucky, this) a helicopter full of anthropologists from Johns Hopkins who thought it would be a hoot to pal around with a missionary woman for a while. (Some anthropologists they were, too. One of them asked why I wasn't wearing my habit. I asked him if I needed to explain to him the difference between the Baptists and the papists, and he held up his hand as if to say, "The vocabulary offends." In my mind, he says it with a British accent, but we're hard up for fun around here. In truth, his talk was Chesapeake Bay all the way.) All told, Ervin, and even with all the rushing around, this errand of yours cost me almost three weeks. I'd say you owe me, but I guess you can't owe me if I didn't come back with anything.

The Koulèv-Ville mission is in surprisingly good shape. I say surprisingly, because since the Duvaliers fled on that plane (smuggled out a little peasant girl with them, they did!, to do the cooking and cleaning no doubt), very little that has been in any way associated with the regime has been left untouched. All the way from the airport, through the city, through Pétion-Ville, Henri (their driver) pointed out the various signs of carnage. The burnt shell of a building here, the bourgeois house overrun by shanty people there. It made me fear for what I would find, because tensions in the country are still running high, and even in Okap it was known that Brother Joe had dealings with the regime.

But you and I know Brother Joe was a shrewd man, and he had his people do a shrewd thing. When the lawlessness flared up, instead of hunkering down right away, they first dragged much of their excess food and sundries outside—bags of rice, cooking oil, salted meats, vegetables—and let the people take them, knowing what goodwill would follow. Where Brother Joe went wrong, I would say, is in miscalculating the limits of that goodwill. This was a failing, I believe, to which he was prone, expecting big goodwill when all you are is a person who invites a little goodwill. Down there by the hospital are rows of mango trees, where me and Ed spent some pleasant hours back when I was young and Ed was still alive. That's where I expected to find this Sheila, bent semi-comatose over old Sam's grave. But all I found there were those two pet monkeys they used to keep in those tiny cages before they dismantled the mission zoo. They wore harnesses, and they had been tied to the tree trunks by the old man who parades them in the street with their tin beggar cups whenever any work groups—American or Dutch, he does not discriminate—are in town doing their good deeds. It's a real breach of protocol, not to mention security, that the monkey man could get away with a thing like that, and it never would have happened in Brother Joe's day. Nor would there be a hole in the mission wall near the garbage dump, so people could reach in and grab the trash bags and dump them on the property next door and claim their chicken bones and whatnot. Nor would there be dirty hospital needles in those bags like the ones I found among the wads of befouled toilet paper, the discarded food wrappers, the slit-cut burlap rice sacks I watched children carrying away at the direction of their mothers. Brother Joe would have stood over the shoulders of the orderlies as they dug a pit, built a fire, burned everything infectious, covered the hole with the dirt they had just finished digging. If he so much as saw something so useful as a burlap sack in a garbage can, he would have fired the cook on the spot, and made somebody's wife finish making the meal.

When I got back from the mango trees and the graves and overseeing the dreary work of cleanup and the business of reuniting monkey with master, I marched into Larry Garvey's office and said, "Where is she?" He just shrugged his shoulders and pointed vaguely in all directions. I met T. C. Johnson out in the co-op fields, and I said, "Where is she?" He turned his palms toward the sky and said, "Last time I saw her, she was headed toward the village." I walked out into the village by myself and I asked all the women, and they would speak with me of everything but the girl. I walked all the way to the next town. No one would talk there, either. It was getting dark by then, and if I had any regard for my own life I wouldn't have been out walking those mountain paths by myself, anyway, but, Ervin, this country has made me a tough old broad, and I like to think I could hold my own with any two machete-wielding teenagers.

Somewhere between the Pentecostal church and the old French fort, a woman with whom I had spoken earlier in the day, name of Jilene, stepped out of her house and took my arm and walked with me for a while. At first I thought she meant to be protective of me, but then she said, "You are looking for Madame Samuel?" and I said I was, and she pointed toward a house a few hundred feet away and said, "Do not bring her any more sadness." Then she kissed me on both cheeks and we parted.

The house was made of stone and mortar, with a roof of corrugated tin with holes rusted through at irregular intervals. Here and there, the holes had been patched by laying a square of tin or aluminum on top and anchoring it with a large loose rock. Probably underneath the rock, inside the house, was a floor full of pots and basins strategically arranged to catch the rainwater. I've seen it plenty before. The outside of the house had been long ago painted a thick green, but time had washed the color thin at the mortar, and thinner where the stones protruded. Mortar and stone alike were dirtwashed and claywashed. Here and there the gray and orange overtook the green, so there was a shag carpet effect when you saw the place from a distance. An old dirty shag carpet from the floor of somebody's doghouse, let's say. I could only imagine what it was like on the inside.

Nobody answered when I knocked, but I could hear whispering inside, and soft clattering. I knocked again, and it got quieter. I knocked a third time, and the door opened a crack. I saw a white eyeball in a black socket. A man spoke to me in a broken-down English that sounded like Kreyol: "What do you want?"

The girl, I said. Is she here? Will she come talk with me? I came from Okap to see her. People are worried about her. Can I come inside?

"Wait," the man said. He closed the door. More whispering inside. Perhaps some arguing. The door opened again, and the man came outside. He was tall, for a Haitian, and handsome. "There is no one here," he said.

"But there is," I said. "I heard the voices inside."

"That is my family," he said. "My brother, my sisters."

"Are you a Christian?" I said.

He allowed that he was.

"Do you mean your brother and sisters from your father and mother, or do you mean your brother and sisters in Christ?"

He looked around, up and down the street. People were watching. He said, "This is not your country."

I switched to Kreyol. "For many years it has been my country," I said.

"Look at your skin," he said. "You are a *blan*. This is a country of *nèg yo*."

"You are a Christian," I said. "Do you know the Scripture, the words of Bondye spoken through the Apostle Paul? In Christ there is neither Jew nor Gentile, neither slave nor free, neither male nor female."

"And yet," he said, "the missionaries have everything and we have nothing. Look at me. Look at where I live. I live very well, but next to the mission, I have nothing."

"Is that what you desire for her, then?" I said. "To have nothing, like you say you have nothing? She is missing, and she is far from home. Her husband has died. Her mother, her father are worried about her."

He scratched at a scab near his temple. "Her husband was a brother to me," he said. "He baptized all my children. He paid for medicine for my mother. He told me if I died, he would take care of my family."

"What is your name?" I said.

"They know my name at the mission," he said. Already he was going inside. Already he was closing the door.

I put my foot between the door and the doorpost. He drew himself to full height. I said, "Sheila, honey, are you in there?"

"Please," he said. "Do not put your foot in the door."

I called out: "Sheila? Are you in there? My name is Linda Reelitz. I have letters from your mother and your father. I have documents from Brother Sam. There is property that is yours in Florida? Did you know? There are people who love you, Sheila, and they are worried about you."

Nobody made a noise inside. The man put his foot against mine. He did not kick or push at my foot. He said, "Please, now you will go away."

What else could I do? "Sheila," I called. "I will be back tomorrow. Let's talk tomorrow morning, okay?"

I took my foot away from the doorpost. He looked at me for a moment. What I read on him was mostly relief. He closed the door softly. I walked back to the mission in the darkness, alone.

A late-night staff meeting was hastily convened. I described the shag carpet house, and Brothers T.C. and Larry right away exchanged one of those *Didn't we know it?* looks, and in unison, like some quarter-throated choir, everyone in the room said *Kenel*, by which, I learned, they meant Kenel Depitor, a co-op farmer who had been close with Brother Sam. I asked the questions you'd expect: What's going on here? How long's she run off? Why this Kenel Depitor? What's the relationship here? Is this a mere friendship, or might she have waded into something sexual?

Nobody seemed to know what to say, right off. Faces drew tight. Shoulders were shrugged. Glances, seemingly meaningful, were exchanged, but not with me. Eye contact of that sort was rare as a seven-dollar bill. Things were said that didn't mean anything: It's hard to know, it's complicated, Sheila's a tough nut to crack, Sam could be a weird egg.

"Listen," I said. "You people have been through a lot. Lord knows. You've lost a lot of people you love. Good people. In a short time. And here's your last link to one of them, this girl who got dropped on you even though you probably didn't want her, but here she is, and she was Sam's, and you loved Sam, and Sam is gone, and she's all you've got left of Sam. So you've got your loyalty to Sam, and you don't want to hurt this girl, and neither do I. Neither does anybody. But there's stuff going on here that doesn't smell right. I've seen it all, and now I've got the spiritual gift of seeing through it all. I watched my Ed's head crushed between the cab and the bed of an old pickup truck, and I watched my housekeeper fall off the side of a cliff with her house back when we still lived in the mountains. I don't know what to do with any of it. All I know is there's this girl, and one way or another she's in over her head, and we've got to get her home so she can make some kind of life for herself and not have everybody just thinking of her as the widow at the ripe old age of fourteen or whatever she is."

I went on like that for a while, just provoking. It didn't hurt me one bit to do it. I just beat on them like that. When an English word wouldn't do, I used a French word, and when French wasn't crude enough, I hammered them with Kreyol. I played the tired old widow and I played Ervin's monster come down from the north to chew and spit. Finally, Sisters Patty and Thelma started talking a little. Yes, they said, Sam *was* a weird egg. Yes, Sheila *was* a tough nut to crack. It's not that they knew things and were choosing to withhold them from me, their interrogator. They *didn't* know, and it's what they didn't know that wore them at the edges. What they had to offer was gossip, idle talk, conjecture, theories half-formed. What they had was nothing edifying. What they had wasn't much. That's why the hemming and that's why the hawing.

"Ladies," I said, "if theory's all we got, then theory's all we got."

The long silence. Then Patty: "Kenel and Brother Sam were very close."

Like brothers, Thelma said.

"After Sam died, Kenel started to come around a lot more. Usually he kept to his fields, and that's where he spent his time with Sam. But after Sam died, he was always bringing baskets to Sheila. Food, clothing, things he bought or his wife bought at the market."

"Things he couldn't afford," Thelma said. "Not possibly."

"Did you ask Sheila about these things?" I said.

"Yes," Patty said. "Indirectly, but that didn't get anywhere. Then directly. But she was just a mess. Her face turned witch ugly. It took so little to set off the waterworks. Once it started, she'd go off to her bedroom and shut the door, and you'd hear her for hours. She wouldn't answer if you knocked. Such a horrible sound, and you could hear everything that came out of that room anyway, because the walls were so thin, and because of where it was. So we just stopped asking."

"Where do you think he got the money?" I said. Their speculations were thin. Maybe she had some stashed away, and Kenel came and got it and made purchases on her behalf. Maybe Sam left some of his money with Kenel. It was no secret the troubles were coming. It was just a matter of when. Maybe he thought he ought to have a backup plan if this place got tore up. I said these were reasonable possibilities, and that's why I didn't buy them. They believed something darker, and might as well be out with it. They looked at each other. The men glared at the women. I had a pretty good idea what the women were going to say.

"We think maybe Kenel was his backup plan," Patty said.

"But Kenel has a wife," I said.

"Kenel has three or four wives," Patty said, "stashed away who knows where."

"What's one more?" Thelma said.

By now, the men had stopped glaring at them. Some leaky water pipe was dripping every few seconds, and the men turned their heads in the direction of the showers every time a drop hit the drain. The women seemed to be waiting for the men to say something, and I waited them out. They fiddled with their ears and they fiddled with the creases in their pants. Finally T. C. gave in. "It's just a theory," he said. "It's just talk, and it's not kind, and it's probably not true."

I didn't have to say it was midnight, and Sheila was in Kenel's house, and not in her own bed, and not for the first night, I gathered.

Well, Ervin, this story doesn't end well or end at all, for that matter. The next morning I set off with Patty and Thelma for Kenel's house. When we got there, the door was open, the bedsheet curtains were gone from the windows, the inside was picked bare. Everybody and everything that was there was there no more. We interviewed the neighbors, and the neighbors were predictably ignorant concerning these matters. We interviewed the relatives, and nobody had a thing of value to share with us. Somebody said maybe they went to Jacmel, somebody said Belle Anse, somebody else said Miragoâne. All of these were places none of these bodies have ever been, I can assure you. If I had to guess, I'd say they're all some place three mountains over, sharing some uncomfortable space with some children Kenel hasn't seen since they were born.

What to do? I guess you could call the FBI kidnapping squad if you want, Ervin, and let Kenel Depitor take a bullet for the crime of doing a favor for his dead friend. They call us colonialists, and that's what anybody'd expect, right? My advice is wait it out. Soon enough, the money will run out, or she'll get homesick or she'll get sick sick, and one fine afternoon she'll walk or be carried through the front gate, dehydrated and weak with diarrhea, and one of those nurses will run an I.V., and then T. C. and Larry will send her stateside. As for me, I want to wash my hands of the whole sorry affair. What I want to know is: What kind of man was Brother Samuel Tillotson, anyway? And what was Brother Joe thinking, letting him bring that girl here in the first place? And what kind of girl is she, to get mixed up in a distant country with one man she hardly knew, and now another? And what kind of parents must she have, to let us deal in fact-finding trips and bureaucratic reports instead of getting their old behinds down here on a plane and bringing their little girl home? And what kind of people are we, in a time like this, to let her grieve it out alone in that thin-walled bedroom? Why wasn't she put on the morning plane to Miami the day after Brother Sam was buried?

As usual, the questions pile up like dug dirt, and the big ditch forms for lack of answers. Days like these I want to throw myself in it and sleep the long sleep, but that's not what we do. As soon as I'm

able, I'm gonna get myself back to Okap and lead some Bible stud-
ies and oversee some women's meetings, and plant some trees, and
teach some children to read.

V.

Mrs. Tina Brocken, Loxahatchee, Florida, to Miss Anna Ratliff, West
Palm Beach, Florida, May 10, 1993.

Im so sorry to here the news about your daddy passing after such
a long and bravery struggle. I dont even know if you remember me
because you was so little when we knew your daddy. We knew your
momma too and she might remember us. If she does, you say hey
to her for us and you tell her we dont care what anybody says we
think she is a fine person. She was always a good lady to all of us
even though there was problems between her and your daddy thats
the things that happens to everybody in the world and when you
get older you will know it too. You are an adult now so you like to
already do but thats neither here nor there. Kay-Sara-Sara, like that
old French song goes.

    I <u>will</u> do my best to write all the things I want to say to your
daddy in this letter. I want you to forgive me for not coming to the
funeral service to say them for my own self and to his face. There
is a lot of reasons for it. Some of them are because I don't go to the
Baptist church anymore even though I still believe in God and pray
in Jesus name. I have gray in my hair people dont gossip probably
like they used to or even remember me but maybe some do I dont
like there stairs when I pass by and what they are thinking about
me and what kind of mother is walking by them when I walk by.
Also I am not a disrespectful person especially to somebody like
Leslie Ratliff when I first heard about the brain cancer I just cried
and cried you can ask anybody around because they all heard me.

Not just because I felt sorry for him with his pain or but because it really is such a blow to loose him we loved him so much.

Let me start at the beginning because I know your daddy was a discrete man and wouldnt tell everybodys business so you might not know. We had a daughter. Her name was Sheila. When she was born she was the love of our life mine and her daddy too. She was bad sometimes and got into things but thats how children do and she wasnt any different. We didnt have much trouble with her until she got to teen age. Even then she wasnt so bad but just wanted to wear makeup a lot of dark makeup around her eyes thick blue eye shadow and red lipstick and so forth. She was never one to mouth off but some kinds of rebellion are silent like the preachers say the devil doesnt come dressed up in a red Halloween suit he is more like to be the man in the suit and tie on the airplane real handsome with his hair slicked back and two hundred dollar shoes. Well Sheila was very pretty and spoke good to everybody and cleaned up nice and dolled up she was a prize fit for a movie star actor or a tv anchorman or a rich man which I admit to thinking back then that Sheila was just going to catch the eye of one of those boys in her class from Palm Beach who was going to be a doctor or lawyer or inherit a business and I could just see us out there visiting maybe taking one of those yachts to the Bahamas because that is something her daddy had in common with a lot of those guys with the yachts is he was and is a very good watercraft man. People who are into watercraft know who is able and who is not able and you get respect that way no matter how much money you have or dont have and I know it because we have ended up on boats with people like that and it always worked out okay even though it made me a nervous wreck because you always wonder what people like that think about a hairdresser and a Sheet Metal Technician II nearly to Sheet Metal Technician I certification.

So we could of went on like that and everything turned out okay like it does for other families whose daughter wants to wear some makeup or hoop ear rings or a short skirt like many do since we might be in the Last Days before Armageddon and Jesus riding on the white horse to rapture the living and the dead in Christ will rise first. But one day a mimeograft paper comes home from school about the senior trip. Sometimes the senior class goes to Europe but this senior class the note said is a very special one and they the students voted to make theirs a service and missions trip to the poorest most backward country in the world which is right in our backyard Haiti you see on the tv the black people men women children washing up half naked in the rick kitty boats and running from the police and hiding in the bushes the ones who werent able to get away.

Sheilas daddy and me thought there was pros and cons of going to Haiti and not Europe. On the one hand it would be a good cultural uplifting experience to see Paris and London and Big Ben and the Eyeful Tower and that one class a few years back got to go to Omaha Beach where Sheilas granddaddy almost died fighting for our freedom that would be a good thing to see. On the other hand it would be very expensive to ride the airplane over there across the ocean. They have these chicken barbqs to raise money for kids who arent rich like most of the kids but every year I watched those kids sorting dirty t-shirts for the rummage sale and their parents marking notebook paper price sheets for the silent auction items and on the day of the event the same kids and parents up there with the teachers people like or dont like in the clown dunk tank or running the duck pond for the little kids or the ring toss or whatever and all the while you see those rich kids and their parents running around like life is easy and spending the money on the expensive rummage like one year I saw this boob doctor from Palm Beach buy a real nice baby grand piano for his church then strut around like he was the Warren Buffit of charity and filanthropy, and everybody knew that his money was going to pay for some kid not much different from Sheila because of the in adiquacy of some parent like me and Sheilas daddy. Nobody wants to be made to feel that way.

It didnt matter anyway because once Haiti is where the class was going thats where Sheila was bound and determined she was going and I was not one to stand in her way. Her daddy neither. So I just signed the papers. Right away Principle Ratliff called to say there was a special senior trip scholarship fund nobody knew about so we had to keep it quiet but would we like to take advantage of it. This was not the first kindness of your daddys we had seen. I dont want you to think we were poormouthing him. We had money coming in from two jobs but tuition was not cheap at the Good Shepard Academy.

The school sent home all these lists of items to buy. Pack heavy and leave light they said. All those little Haitian kids didnt have toys so we packed some Matchbox cars and bored games and some baby dolls. We bought a pair of cheap underpants for every day the idea being to use them one time and then give them away so some Haitian lady could have a new pair of her own after it got washed. We bought packs of cheese crackers and pop tarts in case a snack was needed because it was dangerous to eat the street food and there wasnt enough at the mission to go around except for regular mealtimes.

You should of seen all those kids lined up at the airport in Miami with all there luggage and backpacks and laughing and horsing around. Me and Sheilas daddy both took the day off work and went down there to see her off. Your daddy was there too with his clipboard playing his role of principle just making sure everyone was accounted for and handing out these little hard candies butterscotches and peppermints and also some caramels to everybody just to make a nice mood. We watched that plane go up in the air through the window by the gate. Sheilas daddy said this was a big turning point in our life because soon she would be gone to college or married or both. I said she would not be our little girl anymore and he said she will always be our little girl. She will never stop being our little girl. He wasnt ashamed his eyes got wet. That wasnt like him. If you ever met him you would see a man with green navy tatoos and a weightlifter and a blackbeard just a big man some would say intimidating. That was part of who he was its true. But he was a daddy foremost and thats what killed him if I get to lay blame.

We knew while they stayed over there we wouldnt here much from the kids. Sheila only got to call us one time for about three minutes the connection was bad and it costed us fifteen dollars. She said it was so lovely the retarded children were lovely and the pregnant girls. Just to here her voice was reasuring. You know thats an island where people are fleeing from danger so you worry about violence and all that. But nothing like that happened where they were. They didnt see anything like that. She felt safe over there and maybe it would of been better if she had got a scare while she was on that senior trip.

She was real quiet when she got home but also somehow lit up like a fire beetle. You know how teen agers are moody and girls especially. We got used to that and tried to be understanding. But when Sheila got back from that trip she like to floated from cloud to cloud even if she was just vacuuming the living room. Twitterpated is what her daddy said. I agreed but there wasnt a single boy calling the house. One day I just came out and asked her and she got shy and wouldnt say very much. But after graduation I knew she was going to William Jennings Bryan College with a full scholarship even room and board then all of a sudden she said she was going to stay home and go part time to the junior college. That was worrisome, her walking away from an opportunity like that. She clammed up about why but we were for sure it was a boy.

Then one Saturday morning the third week of June there was a knock on the front door. I looked through the curtain liked I used

to do and it was your daddy. That was weird for the school principle to be at the door after your daughter already graduated. I called
everybody to the living room then I let him in. He was wearing a two
button shirt and corduroy pants, and I remember thinking that was
funny because it was hard to imagine him in anything but a suit and
tie and penny loafers. I offered him some tea and we all sat on the
couches in the living room to talk. It was small talk for a while and
then he said to Sheila would she excuse us for a few minutes. Her
face was red flushed the whole time he was there then it got redder
when he said that. Her daddy said Sheila you better get on to your
room. After she left he said what kind of trouble has my daughter
got into.

Your daddy had a real nice way with people. He said you know
sometimes its not the children who get into trouble but the adults
who might get them into some. He said something has happened
but I am not sure exactly what or how much of it. It took him a long
time to get into it but the long and short was that one of the missionaries in Haiti was an old school buddy of his from Apalachicola
Bible College and maybe thats what blinded him to what must of
been going on between this older man and our Sheila. He said this
missionary man had wrote a letter saying would your daddy come
talk to us about how him and our daughter were in love from only a
few days together and then it all made sense to me why Sheila was
acting like a lovesick fool and not taking her scholarship and room
and board at William Jennings Bryan College.

Right away Sheilas daddy got up and started pacing the room.
Principle Ratliff said if it was his daughter he would want to punch
somebody in the mouth for being the bearer of bad news but he
would refrane because of his love for God. But something we had
to consider now that Sheila was eighteen and legally an adult was
something could come of it. He asked did we think she was motivated
enough to do something rash? Her daddy said _he_ was. Principle
Ratliff said that was another matter but he understood well enough

because he had a daughter of his own, and here Anna you should know he went on and on about his love for you even then when you was so little he was thinking about when you would be grown and married he would be so proud of you but he wanted it to be somebody your own age or a little older who loved you and you loved. We said that was what we wanted for our daughter too.

We called Sheila into the living room and told her in front of your daddy and all of us what he had said and was it true? She was slippery about it. She said that this man Brother Samuel she had met was very nice and they had got close but no closer than very close friends. Nothing unto ward had happened. Principle Ratliff said he had a mimeograft letter he would give to us so we could see what Brother Samuel had said and from here on out he would leave the matter to our family to make some choices about but he would help if he could he just didnt know what more he should do about it telling us was the right thing to do he thought.

I must have read that letter a hundred times since then including one time today. That letter is really what got so much of this thing off the ground between Sheila and Samuel Tillotson. One day I came home and saw her reading it and she was cucumber eyed like she had been getting. I said that is poison and fire you are playing with and she acted like it wasnt. At that age you know everything or think you do.

A couple of times the phone rang and she answered it then said a few words like she was speaking code. After that she would leave the house all the time. Later we found out she was going to my sisters house her aunt Glory that traitor. Over there she was talking to Samuel long distance Lord knows how much it was costing him or how he was paying for it. What we know now is they were making their plans. One day she was there in the kitchen cutting carrots and the next day she was gone. He swooped in on the airplane and took her up to his brothers house in north Florida and they came back married and saying they were moving to Haiti in two days.

At the time what I thought was what can I do about it now? What is done is done. Marriage has always been sacred to us we are belivers in Jesus. Now I am more sophisticated about my thinking on it. Now I think my daughter was just a child and you cant make a child enter into a binding agreement she was manipulated into. We should of pushed for an annulment like her daddy wanted and put our foot down and said no way are you leaving the country no way with that man old enough to be your daddy with salt and pepper hair and crows feet at the corners of his eyes and his teeth gone so yellow already. But then I just thought what can you do? She was already a year older than I was when I married her daddy.

We said stay at our house then even though it was strange but they had already got a room at the Holiday Inn on Okeechobee Road the same place where her daddy and me had our honeymoon so that was a strange thing to ponder all those memories and think of what was going on in that hotel room. So we took them to a very nice expensive dinner at the Red Lobster to celebrate the wedding we had not been invited to or told about. That was very hurtful even though it saved a lot of money I always wanted to give Sheila the kind of wedding like I never had with a big white cake and a train for her dress and I was going to do her hair up in a tiara and spend a lot of time getting it just right like nobody did for me. A church wedding and not a reception in the church fellowship hall but a real banquet hall someplace like in the movies.

I was real proud of Sheilas daddy during that dinner he leaned over to Samuel Tillotson. He was trembling which is as unusual as tears for him or it was then. He said now that you are a part of our family I want to welcome you into it and you are like a son to me. Which was funny because they were about the same age. He said I just want one thing from you and thats you take good care of my daughter because she is the only thing we got in the world worth a tinkers dam we dont even care about the house or the cars its just her we would give anything in the world for her and you should feel the same way. And Samuel to his credit said that he did feel the same way and we should all feel good knowing that Sheila would be very loved. Right then he put his hand on both our shoulders and prayed there in the restaurant for the family we were becoming to each other. That was embarrassing for us but it would of been impolite to say so because this seemed like a real important moment for all of us. Plus we wanted everything to be nice since Sheila was leaving and it might be a while before she could get back home to see us.

We drove them to the airport. They sat in the back seat and held hands. I didnt like the way Sheila was dressed for the trip a little tarty but I tried to keep it to myself because she was leaving like I said. I had made sure she had all her comfort things she needed and things to do her hair curling irons and so forth. I kept thinking something was missing and later I relized it was some of her stuffed bears she slept with every night until then that her uncle Frank got her when she was little for Chrismas one year. At the terminal there she said Sammy I am hungry can you bring me something? Her daddy like to leaped up to run get her a sandwich. He brought back four sandwiches and four ice cream sandwiches. Her pretty mouth was chewing. Her mouth was always so pretty. I saw Samuel looking at her mouth like a wolf but what could I say I couldnt say nothing they was married.

Her daddy was always quiet but he got more quiet. There was a plane that went down sometimes from the missionary flights international sometimes we brought down some packed boxes with cheese crackers, magazines, granola bars, fresh underwear to give the old ones to those Haitian ladys and pass the goodwill along. I always wrote a letter too but Sheila didnt write back very much. When she did it was short and she just wanted something like feminine products which I was happy to send the next box. One day your daddy called and said its Principle Ratliff but we can be friends now so just call me Leslie and thats what we called him from then until the day he died. He said what can I do and I told him there was nothing to be done about our daughter whats done is done but my husband has got very quiet.

A few days after that your daddy knocked on the door again it was early evening. He told Sheilas daddy he heard we was going to put an addition on our house. Sheilas daddy said that was no longer because the addition was for a guest room for visiting grandbabys and no body of that discription was going to visit us now they just planned to stay overseas always. And your daddy, Leslie, he said time has a way of working these things out. He was very gentle. He said he knew a few things about construction. He was good with electrical work and he could knock out walls with hammers and crowbars and he could hang dry wall and he could lay all kinds of floors from tile to laminate to wood or even carpet.

Every Saturday for eight months after ward he came over and helped Sheilas daddy with that addition. We lived with a open house for a long time. Just Visqueen hanging over the open part to protect from the wind and rain. When we was both gone to work or shopping or church the old jewish lady two houses catty corner from the mailbox was agreeable to watch over the house so no robbers saw no one was home and stole from us. We got a dog too. Big Doberman named Sweetheart. Sweetheart loved your daddy. Thats another way of knowing how good a man he was because guard dogs know bad people.

Almost two years that guest room sat finished and empty. We bought a bed to put it in there but no body slept in it. One day on the six o clock news came word that Baby Doc Duvaliay was fleeing from a cooday taw. We heard there was un rest but the reports now got bad. Somebody at the Baptist church brought over some articles from the Miami newspaper which covered Haiti a lot because of all the Haitians living there and sure enough it was bad enough we got worried. Sheilas daddy said he was going over there on the first plane but the missionary board called and said no planes were getting in and dont go over any way it could put Sheilas life in danger if not handled right the customs being different over there and kind of savage with bribes and extortions possible.

Her daddy stopped going to work then. I called the boss who was an old friend and he said dont worry do you need money and I said we had some saved. He said if his daughter was in trouble over-seas he would wait by the phone and they had sheet metal men to cover the hours dont worry. Sheilas daddy stopped sleeping in our bed. He went into that empty guest room and just sat there on the bed. I told him he was going to rot in there and not do any good. He said he was waiting for the next knock on the door with the sheriff or some missionary saying his daughter was dead. I told him dont talk like that you have to have faith. He got real cold then and said havent you figured out by now it doesnt matter how much faith you have the same bad things happen to Christians as pagans. I said I know I have seen the same things as you.

There was that knock on the door. It was a week later. I heard her daddy there in the guest room. He said shes dead our daugh-ters dead. I said its probably some kids selling worlds finest chocolate bars for the school money drive trying to win first prize of a black and white tv. He said if its somebody in a suit then you will know.

Who it was was Leslie. Sheilas daddy said he wasnt coming out of the guest room. We all went in there and sat on the bed the three of us. Its bad news he said. She is dead, Sheilas daddy said. Leslie said no shes not but Samuel is. Sheilas daddy closed his eyes. He didnt make a sound but there was tears shooting down his cheeks. That son of a bitch he said. Leslie put his arms around both of us even though he was not a hugging man. We told him we ought to go down there and get Sheila. He said dont do it let her grieve the loss her own way let the authorities at the missionary bored han-dle sending her back who knows what shes liable to do in her grief if we show up there.

This made me angry. I am her mother. I am the one whos

supposed to be with her when she is grieving. I dont care if shes in Haiti or Timbuktu or if the plane ticket costs three thousand dollars or you have to fly on the back of a bird. I said we are going its settled. Your sweet daddy said I dont blame you. He opened his billfold and gave us some money. We wrote some letters and sent them down with the missionary flights plane. We bought some tickets and went down there as soon as they opened the airport for comercial flights. There was a hundred people outside the gate wanting to give us a ride in their taxi which was probably a run down car or pick up truck. These people smelled to high heaven. They dont wear deodorant down in those places. We chose this one short little fellow who had all his teeth and spoke English. His name was something like Ornery but I dont think thats how its spelled. We asked him if he knew the Baptist Mission in Koulèv-Ville and he said he had a cousin who used to be a cook there.

He put us in his pickup truck all three of us in the cab together. The roads were terrible. People were walking between the cars in the streets trying to sell you things through the window it was terrifying. The buildings were all cinder block painted some god awful color pink or green or yellow sometimes with a picture painted on the side or some words in French. There was a lot of places that had been tore down very recently. You could tell because people were picking in them for food or whatever was inside, scavenging like vultures. What kind of country is this I wanted to know. I was so happy we had come to take our daughter home.

We gave the driver some money at the mission gate but he said it wasnt enough. We tried to haggle but he acted like he didnt understand and he kept saying I gave you the ride why wont you give me the money? Some other Haitians came around trying to sell us trinkets and paintings and others were saying you are thiefs. Finally a white man came out and saw us and said who are you and what are you doing here? I said we are the Brockens, our daughter lived here, she was Sheila Tillotson. When he heard that he took

money out of his pocket and gave it to the driver and started talking
to everyone in that Creole and some people were arguing but he sent
them away and took us inside.

I need to make this long story shorter. This is supposed to be a
letter about your daddy and I am going on too long about this but
this is part of the story okay. They brought us out all this food but
Sheilas daddy said he didnt want to eat anything in this god for-
saken country he just wanted to see his daughter where is she. He
went storming around yelling Sheila Sheila, and it took a while to
get him calmed down. They took us back into a back room. I said
shes not here. One of the women said no shes not. Where is she? The
woman said she didnt know. Is she alive? These are the questions
any mother would want to know. The woman said as far as we know.
She was not un kind. She was trying to be calm but she was upset
as us. Sheilas daddy said tell us what you know. The woman started
to talk but the man said we just got there we should rest. Sheilas
daddy grabbed him by the shirt and said you tell us what you know.
The man put his hands on Sheilas daddys hands but what can you
do? Sheilas daddy had sheet metal arms. The man said okay al right
you tell him to the woman who I gather was his wife. The wife said
I dont know how to say this but she ran off with this Haitian man
Kinnel who was friends with Samuel. Shes been gone a few days
and we dont know where she went. We didnt know this would happen we are so sorry. Sheilas daddy said this Kinnel is a black man?
He is Haitian the woman said. Sheilas daddy said when you say run
off do you mean escaping danger or site seeing or romantic or boy-
friend girlfriend or get married? And the woman said theres no way
to know for sure but we think romantic by now. Shes very confused
shes been thru so much.

What was there to do after that but go home? We stayed the
night in the mission but neither of us slept at all. In the village you
could here some people singing hymns in that Creole. Even though
it was Christian it sounded like the voices of the demon possessed.

The whole country was infested. Somewhere out there I was sure Sheila was singing with them. She was turning into one of them and probably having babies with one of them or made one already because there is no birth control in that country for sure unless you are getting it from Americans and she was out there living like a savage. Her daddy said the same thing in the middle of the night. If she has any babys they are going to be black. That was his last word on the subject. He also said we are never going to see her again.

Your daddy was very good to us after that. He had the ladys at his church cook us meals in a rotation one for every day of the week for a month and bring them to us so we didnt have to worry about the cooking. He visited with Sheilas daddy and he said dont listen to the poison those old bitties are spewing. Just because they go to church doesnt make them spiritual. No person in their right mind can blame you for what choices she has made. If any body is responsible it is me Leslie Ratliff I should of not taken those kids down there my old friend was a snake and I should of known it I should of kept him away from her I should of been more aware. Sheilas daddy said no its not true. What a girl learns about love she learns from her daddy. Theres something I did wrong and I should of known it when. Even those early signs I had a chance. That red lipstick and those hoop ear rings and those short skirts. I said your not leaving this house done up like a two bit whore but I could of put my foot down more. I could of got out the belt or the switch like the bible says spare the rod or spoil the child but I couldnt bare to do it not when she was little and not now and now I am paying the price you sow what you reap. Your daddy was so compassionate he said no no thats not true I have been a principle for many years now and you see all kinds of kids good and bad from all kinds of families good and bad and you know God forgives sins and there is still time for Sheila I knew her she was a good girl even if she had a wild streak. He said you know the story of my wife who left me for the navy captain. She may be a kept woman but I know in my heart God will bring her back to me. She is still my wife in the eyes of God. God will forgive my wife and I will forgive my wife and she will come back to me. And God will forgive Sheila and you will forgive Sheila and she will come back to you. Then we will all sit down and kill the fatted calf and feast like in the story of the prodigal son your family and mine all of us together. The day is coming you will see.

Every Saturday they had this same conversation. Then one Saturday there was some news from the mission. Some body had creeped back from the provinces and said Sheila was dead and they buried her in a family crypt somewhere. They werent telling where. She had got sick and died and everyone was afraid because she was white. There was some debate about whether to send news but finally they did send it out of a heart for her family. But you tell me. If they really had a heart for our family they would say where she died and where she was buried so we could go get her. Those people. But it never happened. We dont know where she is and we dont know if she had any babies. They would be our grandbabys. I would take them now even though they might be black. They would be black but they would still have Sheilas face and some of her features. I would love them the same as I loved her. I am not prejudice. I would raise them to know the lord and go back to church and never let them wear any thick makeup or jewlry. I would work as hard as I had to so I could send them to Good Shepard Academy and give them a good education because its so important. But every day I think they dont even know English and probably cant read or do basic math. That just galls me every day. They are alive and carrying her blood I know it. They will never know my name or that I am there grandma.

If you think it was hard for me you should of seen Sheilas daddy. He lasted 18 months after that. Massive coronary. His heart just exploded. There was surgery but it was to late. The only person who came around after that was your sweet daddy Leslie Ratliff. Oh was he a friend to me. We sat a part on the couch and watched television and some times went to the movies one time he even took me to the musical play Fiddler on the Roof. Lonely days were made less lonely even doing things like watching the Kentucky Derby on tv or baseball then making cookies or sometimes he would help repair the toilet or any thing else that was broke. One day I said to him why dont we get married. We love each other in the right way and never did any thing un toward. We could make a life together. I said I made my peace with my daughter is never coming back. I said your wife is never coming back to you either. He said she is not dead. I said I know but she might as well be dead to you. He said I trust the lord. Well I admire him for that but as you know your momma had made her choices and they were ever bit as binding as the ones Sheila made. But your daddy was not scared off. He kept visiting just as a good friend and I was respectful to the love he still had for your mother and he was respectful to me and treated me like a dear sister in Christ even though I had stopped going to the Baptist church because of those bitties and there gossip.

One thing I never said to your daddy because I never blamed him was how different life would be if no body had invented the mimeograft machine. It was that mimeograft machine that brought home the paper that convinced all the parents to send their children to Haiti instead of Europe. And it was the mimeograft machine that brought the copy of the letter from that terrible Samuel that Sheila always used to sneak off and read and help her fall in love some more and go down the wrong path. Thats something I think about all the time. I was thinking about it today. I was sitting on the bed in that guest room your daddy helped build. Sweetheart was barking. The rest of the house was so quiet I had to go turn on the tv to keep me company. Its what made me think of writing you the letter. I was thinking about that mimeograft machine and it got me thinking of your daddy. He was so special. Every body must of told you by now but I wanted you to know how much he meant to me being here for me in my darkest hour. I wish he would of known God doesnt always answer prayers the way you want him to. Maybe you could of been a daughter to me.

I couldnt take the place of your real momma or your daddy and you couldnt take the place of my Sheila but we could of still been like family to one another. Maybe theres still time.

VI.

Günter Maier, Director, The Committee for Haitian Reforestation, Pétionville, Haiti, to Angela Lopez, Graduate Teaching Assistant, Department of History, University of North Carolina, Chapel Hill, North Carolina, March 19, 1995.

The referendum is in: I will not be visiting North Carolina anytime soon. The Americans give with one hand and take with the other. The sticking point is the guns from El Salvador. They held me for three days and since there was nothing for me to say, I said nothing, and they fed me well enough and gave me a blanket, and I slept like a baby. Eventually, our good friend Nils came down with three men from the German embassy and a Dutch diplomat and three Haitian lawyers, and the good American colonel declared me a free man, but a Jeepload of American soldiers knocked on the door at committee headquarters yesterday and served papers saying I was hereafter barred from flying into Miami or any other port of entry to American soil. I wanted to grab these men by the shoulders and shake them and say, who do you take me for? I'm one of the good guys. I did say to the one, "Have you been to La Saline?" He said he patrolled the road by the market almost every day. I told him to get a good look at that filthy maze of shelters and shanties, imagine some reckless poor man with fifty fresh dollars in his pocket and a rocket launcher on his shoulder. "Look past his shoulder toward the sun," I told him. "There you'll see the flight path of every American Airlines flight that ever landed in Port-au-Prince." He didn't say anything, but he blinked his eyes a few times. I'd heard the stories.

He was probably in a convoy some time that took sniper fire right around the same place. I'm sure he was wondering the same thing I was wondering: What was his government thinking, restoring that crazy communist priest to power? Remember the idiom you taught me that evening in Boutilliers, when we were sipping clairin on that strip of grass overlooking the orange-and-silver glinting of the sun off the rooftops at dusk? "The inmates are running the asylum"? This is what I wanted to say to him, but I was angry, and my mind was full of anger-fueled idioms of every variety—French, Spanish, Creole, German, Dutch, Italian. My English was not close enough at hand, and I could not summon the words I needed to say: You don't take the guns from the good people. You take the guns from the bad people. Or: The last thing this country needs is a democracy. What this country needs is an iron-fisted benevolent dictator. Somebody who will protect the businesses and protect the port and build roads and build up the banking system. Somebody who will refuse to accede to the tyranny of poor people whose every action seems calculated to keep them poor forever. Let me tell you something your professors in North Carolina won't like, Angela: Poor people don't want not to be poor. Poor people just want everyone else to be as poor as they are. That's where we're headed as soon as the Americans leave, I'm afraid, unless our dear president turns out to be a more accommodating fellow than he has proved himself to be in the past.

I wish that was the strangest thing that happened yesterday, but you did your time here. You know how it is. Yesterday we drove to resupply the safehouse in D_____. Sometime around noon three teenage boys came up the street dragging a blue blanket. The blanket was heavy with something. They moved like they were running from something. A second group of boys came yelling. They were carrying machetes and swinging them above their heads. We closed and barricaded the door and watched on the security monitors. The first group of boys dropped the blanket and fled. The second group stopped at the blanket. They kicked at it and poked at it with their machetes. For a while they stood over it and consulted one another. No one who passed on the street looked at them or what they were doing. I had never seen these boys before, but how often do I get to D_____?

After a while we heard the voice of a man screaming. The sound he made was terrible, animal. When his body appeared on the monitor, it matched his voice. It was a wiry, haggard body, muscled and too lean. The man was tall but hunched. He had an overfull beard that curled at its ends. When he came into the frame, the boys began to shout at him and raise their machetes, but they backed away. Then, from the distance, came gunshots. The boys and the man fled alike. We left the video monitor, then, and went into the back of the safe house, where we could achieve a greater distance from the gunshots. We waited until the shooting ended, and then we waited some more.

When we returned to the front room, we looked again at the monitor. The blanket was still lying on the ground, but it no longer carried its burden. Nils asked if the videotape was still running. I checked, and it had ended. We took the tape from the recorder and put it into the VTR in the back room and rewound it. There we saw the men with the guns run past the blanket and past the front of the building and out of the frame. Then we saw the concrete shop and the machine shop across the street taking bullets from both sides of the frame. Two groups of men were shooting at each other. The shooting went on for some time, but not for as long as it had seemed to go on when we were waiting it out in the back room. When it was over, a little boy who could not have been more than seven or eight years old came into the frame. He walked directly to the blanket. His back was to the security camera. We saw him bend down over the bundle and reach in and grab something and begin to pull it out. Slowly—for this child, it was an effort—he came away pulling a pair of arms, a woman's arms, by the hands and wrists. Nils said, "Is that a white woman?" and when her head came briefly into the frame, the hair did not appear to be the hair I had seen on the head of any Haitian. "Maybe she's Levantine Haitian," I said. "Maybe she's Lebanese." There was no way to tell for sure, the quarterframe picture was so blurry.

The little boy dragged the woman's body out the right of the frame, in the direction of the alleys where the squatters have built. Perhaps it was not advisable for us to do what we did, but we opened the front door and walked in the direction from where the boy had come. We walked toward the squatter houses, but when we reached them we did not go any farther. It did not seem wise to go any farther.

When we returned to the safehouse, we watched the tape again and again, but we could not come to any agreement about the woman—was she Dutch? was she Lebanese? was she one of those mythical Polish Haitians everybody's heard about but nobody's seen?—except that surely she was dead. And who was the child? And why was he taking her?

Nils made his jokes: We go to the police. We go to the old macoutes. We go to the CIA. We go to the missionaries. We go to the priests. We go to the American soldiers. But the only place we went was home. I have lived here since I was five years old, Angela, and this country is the only home I really know, but the older I get, the less I understand this place. I hate it that you left, but all night I dreamed about that bundle in the blanket, and I was so happy it was not you.

Please, love: don't return to me.

Q & A

Q: What do you do in heaven?

A: Drink liquor, blow fire, and pray.

Q: Big G doesn't mind?

A: With Big G, you have to make your own fun. The streets are paved with gold and lined with jewels. The sky shines with emeralds, diamonds, and rubies. The buildings are constructed of marbles of greens and reds and the fiercest blue. But the edifices are all facade. The storefronts are empty. Nobody needs to sleep or eat or make money, so nobody has to work or make a home. Big G made us crowns, but all we're supposed to do is throw them at His feet. All the songs are triumphant and resolve to a major key. It's pretty boring after a while.

Q: Why drink in heaven?

A: It's a sad place. The climate is milder than hell, but they get the movies and the hard drugs. I've spent whole decades making carvings of bricks of heroin I can't inject, lines of cocaine I can't snort. All we do most of the time is remember the good bad days, tell stories about them, make books to hold the stories. I once spent a century honing a seventy-ton rock into compliant and foldable pages. I bound them with iron. But most of the time we run

toward acid-free paper. I've written 397 books so far, but that's
nothing. You should see how my friend Joyce works. She writes so
many thousands of books I'm not sure even eternity will be time
enough to read them. It's a grind, if you ask me.

Q: What do you pray for?

A: You always start with the obligatory praises, to butter Him
up. Then you ask for more liquor.

Q: How do you blow fire?

A: Take a big suck of air. Pour 151-proof rum into your
mouth. Hold a fiery torch near your mouth, at a seventy-five
degree angle. Spit for all you're worth.

Q: How does Big G spend His time?

A: Ducking our questions.

Q: What is the purpose of this book?

A: A catalog of stories and sadnesses, beginnings and end-
ings, the stuff of childhood, death. Nothing new can happen here,
so all you do is think about the days of life when possibility hadn't
been ripped from you forever, when anything could happen, and
wonder why so much was squandered, so much wasted.

Q: What things do you remember most often, besides your
sadnesses?

A: My little brother had a hamster named Eddie. We built
him a magical castle made mostly of glass cages connected by plastic tubes, and lined with wood chips we changed every day. We
gave him a kitchen, a bedroom, a TV room, a billiards room with a
bidet, a concert hall, a gymnasium, an art studio, a science lab, a
hall of mirrors, and a room filled with purple smoke. But all Eddie
wanted to do was run his hamster wheel all day. It made a terrible noise. He ran himself to death. He only lived five months. You
should have seen his face in the little shoebox casket. He seemed
relieved.

Q: How does Big G decide who gets into heaven?

A: It's as arbitrary as everything on the earth. No rhyme or

reason, except this: To whom much is given, more will be given. From whom much is withheld, more will be withheld. How long can this go on? Can you help me find a way to end this?

Q: Do you have anything left to say?

A: Only the same things turned over again and again, as though turning them again will bring some new insight. But the new insights are the same as the old insights. Heaven is a hamster wheel.

Why won't my heart stop beating?

SUSPENDED

THE LOCKER ROOM WALLS WERE PAINTED puke green and lined like a cage with metal hooks, and red mesh equipment bags hung from the hooks like meat. One of the bags was swinging, and I was swinging in it, and Drew McKinnick slapped at it and did his punching, and the janitor got me down.

What did my father say to the principal, and how many times had he said how many things? My boy is not eighty pounds yet. My boy is in the seventh grade. My boy is not a linebacker. Can't you see I love my boy? If you had a boy to love what would you not do?

What did the principal say to my father? Did he say he had a boy and the boy got caught drinking in the tenth grade and he kicked his own boy out of school, same as anybody else? Did he tell my father what he told us once a year when they brought the boys into the gymnasium and left the girls away? I loved and love my wife, and she is not my ex-wife, not praise Jesus in the eyes of God, despite her running off with the Navy captain, despite it all I wait and wait and one day she will be restored to me. I know it in my heart of faith, I wait as Hosea waited, now let us pray.

Whatever passed or did not pass between them, this once it did not matter how much money McKinnick's father gave the school, or how many animals he had veterinaried to health, or how many ordinances he had sealed with his mayor's seal. This once I came home beaten and bruised and told my father, "They suspended him for three days."

That night I slept and dreamt of three days free of red ears flicked blood red and slapped until I heard the ocean. The bathroom was mine to piss in, free of fear of footsteps from behind, one hand in my hair and the other on my belt, the painful lifting, then my head beneath the commode water.

That afternoon I skip-stepped to the bus, the Florida sun high and hot, and this once thinking the heat balmy and tropical rather than stalking and oppressive. Then, somewhere between the Route 7 and the Route 8, somebody grabbed me by the collar and slammed me against the black bumper. At first I thought it was him, because it looked like him, same dog teeth, same mocking smile, but bigger somehow, and how had it been kept from me he had an older brother?

"You think you're something," he said, and lifted me until my feet were off the ground. He was as big as my father. "You ever run crying on my brother again, I'll beat you within an inch of your life, you hear me? I wouldn't mind breaking you."

He had me up against the back of the bus, and somewhere somebody had taught him how to do it, and his brother, too. I can see their faces now, but younger, fleshier, their father pressing their bodies to the wall, and then, older, leaner, their sons looking down at their fathers in their fear, learning.

LAY ME DOWN IN
THE BLUE GRASS

MY HANDS HAVE NOT KNOWN MUCH LABOR. I mix oils and acrylics, gouache and watercolor. On this day I don't paint except in my head. I lack the skill for such dark images as my mind invents. The color palette runs to crimson and deep purples, with brilliant yellow and chartreuse accents where shadows should darken. Imagine a Kentucky mountain as a landscape turned to anger and needing to purge by the rushing of waters. Boulders are flung loose from earth, and massive living trees propel forward as missiles and lodge in the sides of steep rock walls.

Idleness is out of place here. My wife and her three brothers contemplate digging a new well. Their father, seventy-three, is driving the lawn-mowing tractor but not cutting any grass. He's pulling my sister-in-law and her two small children in a trailer. He's taking them to the horrible abandoned place where a nineteenth-century barn has crumbled to tangles of moist rotting lumber that used to be a nesting bed for a colony of feral cats, some descended from a stray blooded Persian once owned by my wife. The cats are gone now, and so is Danny, our nephew. Four days ago he walked toward this woodpile with a loaded shotgun and blew off his head. A swarm of flies has taken residence here. The air is thick with decay, and the earth is still soiled with viscera.

•

My wife's youngest brother, Steve, stands thigh-deep in the creek-water and swings a sledgehammer. From my upstream vantage-point he is John Henry, efficient as a piston, chiseled and thick as two grown cedars. Some years ago a layer of concrete was poured above the boulders and bedrock. He pulverizes it with each blow. The water absorbs the powder and washes it down the mountain. He breaks through the concrete to the layer of stone below and keeps swinging. A pile of debris accumulates beneath him. He lifts the shards and rocks, some large as his upper body, and carries them to a shallow place where the water runs faster. He stacks them against the current and says a brief word in praise of beavers, then goes to work shoveling out the filling reservoir behind his dam. He digs past six feet, so deep he can walk the floor and submerge himself.

This is a wild place. Deer run freely and there are no property lines. Brown bears wander these hollows, and even a buck deer can end a man. Poachers run the logging road at night and slip into the darkness. Marijuana plants grow under cover of protected forest, and these gardens are rigged with homemade booby traps meant to maim if not kill. Venomous snakes wander the hills and valleys and take a few dogs each year. My father-in-law owns the top of this mountain and a hundred acres besides on two others, all carved from the Daniel Boone National Forest and bought for a song. A lone logging road bisects the open range of woods and that only because he granted the federal government a ninety-nine-year lease as a hedge against brushfires.

The creek usually runs behind the two farmhouses as a trickle, but sometimes flash flooding accompanies a heavy rain. Once every fifty years the creek jumps its bed and the mountain resurfaces itself in a fit of violence. Rivers used to do this and still sometimes do, despite the best efforts of the Army Corps of Engineers.

This is a Second Amendment place. In the smaller farmhouse where my nephew Danny lived his father Dan keeps two assault rifles, three loaded handguns, several hunting rifles, and the shotgun. Those at least. Other firearms may be stashed in the walls and floorboards. Tables on the back porch are domino-lined with ammunition. Shells are inexpensive and dizzying in their variety. Some bullets can pierce armor and others are made to explode into three hundred fiery pellets on ejection.

Most evenings Dan and Danny sat on the back porch and practiced firing across the creek at a makeshift target range of aluminum cans, glass bottles, and wood cutouts resting on a steel cart. Some nights they hiked upstream to the wooden ruins and shot into them. Just outside the oversize windows overlooking the back porch and the creek beyond and the target range and the pens where Danny kept the golden retrievers for breeding, Dan has hung two homemade bird feeders stocked with sugar water and just enough vanilla to keep the hummingbirds coming back. The smaller bird with the red underbelly is named Meany, and he drives the prettier green-and-gold bird from feeder to feeder, unwilling to share his swill even if it means he will spend the afternoon policing rather than drinking.

We gather by the creek and admire Steve's dam. The children swim in the deep water, and my father-in-law teaches me to skip stones. Smooth, flat, rounded stones without protruding edges tend to fly farthest. The skillful thrower keeps his hand low to the water and parallel with it, and looses the stone with a slight level flick of the wrist. The old man can skip a stone nine times, for a distance of sixty feet. He has been perfecting his technique for almost seventy years. He believes that all things work together for good and has posted the Ten Commandments on his front lawn in defiance of secular courts faraway.

My wife says when she dies she wants her brothers to cut down strong timbers with their axes and build her casket with their hands.

We are to carry her up the mountain, to the high place where she dreamed as a child of building an A-frame log cabin overlooking the valley and where a person with keen eyesight can achieve a vista and survey as much of Appalachia as an olden hill family might have seen in a lifetime. We'll drive our shovels into the soil and let the dirt mix with our sweat and seep into our pores. We'll breathe the dust we have stirred up and lower box and body into the ground with knotted ropes, then take our spades and fill the grave with earth, tamp it down with our feet and plant sod in the spring around the simple marker, here lies Deborah Jayne, remembered by those who loved her. She says grieving must be physical, mourning underscored by exertion.

We will bury Danny tomorrow in the more traditional way, in a Lexington cemetery. The coroner thinks Dan unstable and only yesterday cleared him of suspicion of homicide. In the state capital of Frankfort, the autopsy was conclusive. My father-in-law has inspected every well and septic tank on the property for signs of disrepair. His sons inspect every engine of every car, truck, and van gathered on the grasses between the farmhouses. In grave situations, my father-in-law has been known to counsel the Shalom peace of the Lord to passersby, then pass blood in the privacy of his own bathroom.

At the funeral, lies are told in the name of comfort. Speculations. Maybe it's possible Danny did not mean to kill himself but tripped and discharged the shotgun by accident. The preacher lives by traditions and says we have gathered to celebrate a life and that he's seen some long faces in need of lightening up. He uses biscuits and the ingredients for making them as a visual aid to let us know that a tasty life is made from bitter parts. He gives an old-fashioned call to salvation and not a hand is raised. The reconstructed face in the casket is not recognizable as anything except poorly cast wax. Later his mother says he would have hated the eyeliner and mascara they'd applied to him.

The lies obscure truths we would like to quiet. Danny heard voices under the ground and daily walked outside with his Glock to find and silence them. Some of the hill people say the mountain is riddled with caves and that the older people knew how to get to them but that the old knowledge is dying away as development encroaches upon the old ways. They say that soon there will be no water witchers with divining rods to approach by foot and point out the best places for well-drilling. Danny spent three months in Arizona with some exorcists who claimed demons were whispering in his ears. I believe in the doctors whose antipsychotic medicines Danny regularly neglected. The mind is sufficiently vast for myriad voices to find a place to hide.

Church and cemetery are separated by the greater part of Lexington. Police cars stop traffic for the funeral procession, which is fifty cars deep and slow, in observance of custom. The endless winding from road to road, left turns through red lights and then rights again until an essentially straight path feels circular, leaves me in mind of a hearse-driver perhaps lost with unrelated sadness and leading without benefit of directions or map. The rain starts with droplets at the church steps and turns quickly to downpour in near-opaque sheets. We navigate by taillight.

We wait in our vehicles at the graveside but the rain does not subside. Matt leaves his van and steps into the deluge and beckons the other mourners to follow. Slowly they emerge with umbrellas and ponchos and newspapers held above their heads. Some young people wade unprotected into the falling water and let it soak their clothing to the skin as if their grief required washing or as penance for sins of omission. Maybe they wonder as I do what time spent or what intervention might have changed the course of things.

The rain does not relent as the body is lowered into the grave, nor does it cease during the ninety-minute retreat into the high places. The storm has battered our mountain, and the road to the farmhouses is blocked by fallen timber (the road is in fact named

Fallen Timber Branch Road) and many of the concrete and wooden bridges near the base of the mountain have been swept away by mudslides or washed away by the rising creekwaters.

Nearer the top of the mountain, our cars and trucks dig deep trenches in the open fields. A hundred-year-old cherry tree has toppled and her strong roots point skyward, the ground beneath sucked away by flash flood and gravity. The propane tank has loosed its steel moorings and settled dangerously close to the larger farmhouse. The well is inoperable, its pumps dashed to pieces. The porches are filled with debris spit outward from the rapids. Tall grasses now bend hunched as old men, and the southern field is strewn with loose gravel that once filled a driveway hundreds of yards away. My wife says the mountain itself is grieving. Steve's dam has broken and the waters rush onward toward the valley.

All the breeding dogs have been sold or given away or run off. In a season of speculation, emus were raised from eggs alongside adolescent shelties and golden retrievers in five electrified pens. A spry golden retriever named Mandy mothered nearly half the puppies who grew here. She was the family pet allowed to run free. One evening last autumn she came home with one crippled leg. She's grown white in the face but still runs with her limp after treats of dried beef. Dan is watching her run and I can see it in his eyes: Dogs should not outlive children.

Conversation has ceased and my wife and her brothers have resumed their chores. Last month a local hunter and my father-in-law agreed on a price for the rental of the lower level of his farmhouse to the hunter's daughter and her two college friends. Now the hunter has returned to help clean debris from the common area between the farmhouses and regravel the driveways. All of them strike the ground with their shovels, using more force than their task requires. Mandy cowers beneath an aging car. In the distant woods my father-in-law is alone and talking.

The day Danny was born, Dan saw that the boy had no fingers on his right hand. Dan cursed God and drove away into a storm. He says a bolt of lightning struck a telephone pole and an arc of blue electricity briefly danced upon the hood of his car before dissipating into the ground. Tonight it is dark on our mountain, and we are far enough from the city lights to see the milky plenitude. To be sure, we are hoping for a sign. The distances between stars are now calculable but what passes for mourning is harder to measure. We have photographs and folklore. We have words and hands. We can sell the cherry tree. We can fix the water pump. We can build a new dam. We can dredge a new path for the creek and make it a canal. We can shout out into the quiet of the hollow and hear our own voices echoing: *Ashes to ashes, dust to dust.* The words come back plaintive, longing.

ACKNOWLEDGMENTS

The following stories originally appeared in these publications:

"The Question of Where We Begin," *Gulf Coast*

"You Shall Go Out with Joy and Be Led Forth with Peace,"
   Twentysomething Essays by Twentysomething Writers (Random
   House, 2006)

"The Truth and All Its Ugly," *Fifty-Two Stories* (HarperPerennial
   Digital, 2010), *Surreal South* (Press 53, 2007), in a limited
   edition letterpress chapbook (Bandit Press, 2010), and as an
   Amazon standalone e-book (2011)

"Glossolalia," *Forty Stories* (HarperPerennial Digital, 2012) and
   Cream City Review

"Seven Stories About Sebastian of Koulèv-Ville" (as "Seven Stories
   About Kenel of Koulèv-Ville"), *The Iowa Review* and *Best
   American Nonrequired Reading 2013* (Houghton Mifflin)

"The Sweet Life," *Alimentum*

"First, the Teeth," *Redivider*

"In a Distant Country," *Ninth Letter*

"Suspended," *Brevity*

"Lay Me Down in the Blue Grass," *Mid-American Review*

"Seven Stories About Sebastian of Koulèv-Ville" (as "Seven Stories
About Kenel of Koulèv-Ville") won the 2012 *Iowa Review* Prize for
Short Fiction

The section titles are taken from the Andrew Hudgins poems
"Praying Drunk" and "Heat Lightning in a Time of Drought," both

collected in *The Never-Ending* (Houghton Mifflin, 1991), which all readers should immediately seek out, buy, read, and treasure. The story "Seven Stories About Sebastian of Koulèv-Ville" also quotes from and paraphrases a portion of "Praying Drunk."

Thank you to Lee K. Abbott, Erin McGraw, Ethan Canin, Sam Chang, and Andy Greer—mentors and friends. I am grateful for the ongoing support of Deborah Jayne and Ian and Dylan Minor. I am indebted to Douglas Watson, my first reader and closest editor, and to other friends and editors who helped in some way with these stories: Bart Skarzynski, Joe Oestreich, Okla Elliott, Pinckney and Laura Benedict, Kathleen Rooney, Ian Stansel, Nick Bruno, Jamie Renda, Matt Kellogg, Jillian Quint, Jodee Stanley, Dinty Moore, Philip Graham, Peter Selgin, Cal Morgan, Sophie Chabon, Michelle Herman, Lee Martin, Ron Currie, Aaron Gwyn, Karen Babine, and Mike Czyzniejewski. For crucial help on the publishing side: Katherine Fausset, Steve Gillis, Dan Wickett, Ben Percy, Laura van den Berg, Matt Bell, Kristen Radtke, Meg Bowden, Kirby Gann, and Sarah Gorham. For other varieties of help: Melissa Chadburn, Joyelle McSweeney, Stephen Elliott, Isaac Fitzgerald, Kera Bolonik, Dave Daley, Matt Sullivan, Jen Percy, Phil and Lonnie Murphy, Francky and Tania Desir, Meredith Blankinship, Sarah Smith, Jane Bradley, Ed Falco, Deb Olin Unferth, Daniel Handler, George Singleton, Jan Zenisek, Deb West, Wells Tower, Kevin Brockmeier, Dini Parayitam, Nana Nkweti, Jonathan Gharraie, Colin Kostelecky, Devika Rege, Matt Nelson, Josh Rhome, Hannah Kim, Letitia Trent, Luke Renner, Maureen Traverse, Michelle Burke, Ben Stroud, Karen Kovacik, Robert Rebein, Mitchell Douglas, Terry Kirts, Tom Quach, and Connie Brothers. Thank you.

Miriam Berkley

The Author

KYLE MINOR is a columnist at *Salon, The Nation,* and *HTMLGiant.* His work has appeared in *Esquire, Best American Mystery Stories, Best American Nonrequired Reading, Twentysomething Essays by Twentysomething Writers,* and *Forty Stories: New Voices from Harper Perennial,* among many other publications. He is the recipient of the 2012 *Iowa Review* Prize, the Tara M. Kroger Prize for Short Fiction, and in 2006 was named a Best New Voice by Random House. His previous collection of stories and novellas, *In the Devil's Territory* (Dzanc Books), was published in 2008.